R A D I
Bo

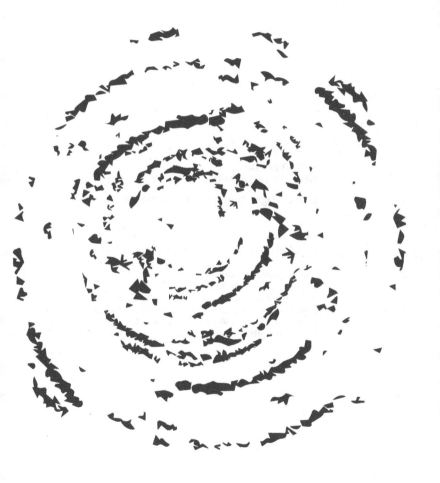

SPUYTEN DUYVIL
New York City

© 2020 Bex Brian
ISBN 978-1-952419-19-5

Cover design: Santiago Garcia Garmaise

Library of Congress Cataloging-in-Publication Data

Names: Brian, Bex, author.
Title: Radius / Bex Brian.
Description: New York City : Spuyten Duyvil, 2020. |
Identifiers: LCCN 2020042787 | ISBN 9781952419195 (paperback)
Classification: LCC PR9199.4.B75 R33 2020 | DDC 813/.6--dc23
LC record available at https://lccn.loc.gov/2020042787

In memory of my mother, Freda.
To my sisters, Tina, Mercy and Sophie.
And, for my husband, Charles.

Faced with a blank wall, I tried to put up a picture. This innate need to give the eye something to snag on felt a little ridiculous. An absurdity doubled, my wall being in a city that exists for no other reason than to fill up space. My first attempt failed miserably when I discovered that here in Abu Dhabi, at least in this apartment, the walls seem to be made of titanium. My nail collapsed under my blows without making a dent. That sort of shocked me, after all, the city is built on moving sands, shouldn't the walls be as porous? I did read the other day that the sand here is too fine to make decent cement for the thousands of buildings being put up all around me, so they have to import the stuff, or, as France is accusing, steal it from their beaches under cover of night. Perhaps they mix in some other element as well. I wouldn't doubt it.

The picture? My sister Frances. She's the only one of my family who I want in the living room.

Later at the mall, looking for a nail with extreme powers, I came across something called Command Strips. That didn't feel right either, this silent mounting of pictures but the wall is now covered with, besides the one of Frances, photos of a man I've been staring at for nearly thirty years. I do have a nice series in what I call the "walking away" pics. C lost in thought, usually playing with his ear, ten, twenty feet in front of me, here in Sicily, there in Iceland, up some mountain, across some field. It's a funny little war, our disparate pace, me lagging, him surging. But good for capturing the great loneliness which we all labour under. I sound bitter, don't I? I'm not. Just girding myself for next week, known, in our family, as

5

"Spiral week." The memory, madness, the heartbreak will come, only I've just never been on the other side of the world before, though I don't see why that should make a difference. The dead are still dead, the missing still missing.

It was my first thought when C came home and said he had gotten a job here teaching the art of narrative science. But after thirty years of freelance writing, of Brooklyn, of boom-and-bust bank accounts, of nights, waking, the two of us side by side yet pretending that the other was fast asleep, the dreads upon us: no future, no money, I couldn't very well say, "What about spiral week? What, if being so far from home, I feel too lonely, too apart?"

I have already aroused some concern among C's colleagues that I, as a trailing spouse, might be unhappy since we chose not to live in campus housing with its cocoon of sociability. It's not uncommon for loneliness to settle like all this dust. Many marriages have faltered. But I am a solitary. I do meet people, young women at the pool who engage me a moment before having to tend to their children. I'm happy to paddle off, though, on occasion, I have bumped into another woman about my age and notice that she too has the same haunted look as me, the two of us aware, in this hologram of a city, of the hum of panic.

It's something I first noticed as I was about to stick up yet another of our framed pictures: this one, a shot taken from our Brooklyn window of an impending thunderstorm with massive cumulonimbus clouds mounting up over Jersey about to march forward and consume a still sunlit Manhattan. Have quite a few weather pictures.

Our Brooklyn apartment has the perfect vantage point. Although, just before we left, I developed a slight fear of heights and found leaning so far out the sixth-floor window unnerving but that's nothing compared to the constant tremor of anxiety that has rumbled through me since we moved here, at times striking me so hard that I have to stop what I am doing and pace around, as if movement could outstrip something like that.

I am a little suspicious of these attacks. Going nuts spiral week, I expect. This feels like something new. Are my feelers picking up an unknown strain muscling into a new quadrant of my brain? Perhaps that's the nefarious underbelly of this place and what I sense in the other women around me, a loss of control. And, perhaps, like me, they also have a murder in the family. Most do, I've learned. Take that, racing pulse and banging heart. Nothing new.

Frances is crooked. How the hell is that possible? For the first time in my life, flat walls, straight lines, clean corners. The first time, too, a washing machine, a dishwasher, and a maid! I've stood at every angle. She's definitely skewed. Gone is any faith in my ability to tell what's straight and what's not. I do feel the heavy condemnation from all the fancy flats around me with their Mercedes, Range Rovers, and Maseratis cooling in the parking garage. "There are people to do that sort of thing." Is there ever! Squads of workers at the ready to do whatever needs to be done, which, has set up a psychic storm in my brain. It's a picture for god's sake. Must I have help? I never have in the past. Lived with slightly crooked pictures, scrubbed my own toilet, made my bed, and walked my dogs. But it feels churlish not to stand dumb before life's chores. These are the rules of this city. If we all did our own dishes, how would a million-plus domestics feed their families?

I was Skyping with Frances last night, me with a drink in hand, and she, a cup of coffee. There was supposed to be a regular trade-off where she got to have the drink and me the coffee, but what with getting plastered every night, I tend not to wake until nine or ten--by then Frances has had her own LA night, found oblivion and is fast asleep. Anyway, as our pixelated facsimiles continuously de- and then re-constituted, Frances, seeing me looking a little sullen around the edges, lost patience and blurted out, "What else do you want?!"

As I roam about this place, Frances' question keeps bobbing up. What do I want? To find a way to quell the raging hysteria and the desire to go haring around this fucked up city blurting out, "piss and shit" all while ripping off my clothes? Maybe. This place certainly brings out that side of me.

Want.

What a question.

My father. What did he want? He wanted to find my sister Lena. End of story. But before that, before everything went to shit, I think all he wanted was to be left alone. He was like a sleepwalker standing on the edge of a parapet, those around him fearing any noise might wake him to his reality; a lousy marriage, his children: one abandoned, one annoying, one too late in the game. Of course, we failed at staying quiet, where's the fun in that? So off the ledge he went, on down into the mosh pit, surviving the family only by matching our mayhem with his thunderous temper.

And Lena? If she's alive. If she's out there somewhere? Does the question of want even come into play? I know one thing for sure, she doesn't want to be found, not by me, or her mother, Liv.

I have a pretty good idea why Frances was so impatient with me last night. It's because she's left dealing with Mother. I'll admit half the allure of moving out here was the twelve thousand miles put between Mother and I rather than a mere two thousand. She exhausts me. There's a woman who's nothing but want. Or was. Now she's a frail nub left only with her barbed tongue. I have wondered if her sharp decline is a physical manifestation of her life of frustration and disappointment. On my last day there, after I had gotten her settled in Frances' backroom, just before I was due to leave she called me in. "You're not a writer, Augati. You're not selfish enough. You're a born nurse." Hard to argue with her when I had just helped her to the bathroom, washed her, changed her and made her toast points, not to mention pack up her apartment—Frances: if she's going to live with me, you have to do everything else—lug all her books and photos up to my sister's and arrange it all in her new room. Taking a seat on the edge of her bed, I looked at her. "I am selfish, Mummy," I said, "I didn't have children so I would never have to be as resentful as you were, or as bored." That got a gleam in her eye.

Had her hands not been so crippled, she might have taken up a pen. But she hasn't written anything in decades. Clearing out her place, I threw out hundreds of folders full of her columns, novels, plays, screenplays, ideas, notebooks. At first, I went through them slowly thinking, at the very least, a few should be saved. But the yellowed, disintegrating newsprint, columns about our family life, all pith and wit, really started to depress me. The meaning was as blanched as the paper. Still, I persisted until I noticed something: Lena was never woven into this public tableau. I started to comb through everything, even her diaries, which, in truth, were mostly appointment books but Lena barely dented those pages. It was bizarre. The time-worn papers in my hands now felt tainted. I looked a madman in that hot little apartment, stuffed with books she never dusted, a kitchen tacky with grime, a life narrowed down to a chair facing a tv, as I, slick with sweat, shovelled a life time's worth of work into green garbage bags. Within an hour, I had filled fifteen bags. Frances was thrilled. "Better you than me." But these past weeks here has given me some perspective, and I can't say that I entirely blame Mother. She wanted a version of a life and Lena was a contrary current: not hers, more rival than step-daughter, and the least inclined to fall under Mother's formidable spell. I sure as shit can't claim the same. I moved to New York to become an actress entirely because that's what mother wanted for me. That I showed no aptitude was not a consideration. I still cringe at the memory of my first scene, the "We of me" speech from The Member of the Wedding which I played with a shimmering menace and howling pathos equal to Brando's overheated Kowalski. Half way through I saw my teacher clutch at his sides in physical pain. Is it any wonder I was tone deaf to Frankie's longing to go with her brother on his honeymoon? All I wanted was to be as far away from my family as possible, though not to vanish off the face of the earth like Lena.

I dropped out before the next class. For a year, I drifted around New York, knowing no one. I'd wake to watch the eleven am movie on PIX and then wander over to the Jefferson Library where I wrote a short story called, "My Memoir Of An Impossible Mother," The final scene has the mother reading her daughter's diary, not only correcting her spelling but leaving notes in the margin. "Is this all you have to report--that you met up with Claire and had cherry cokes and fries with gravy? Unity Mitford at your age had seduced Hitler!"

I sent the story out to magazines on a whim and to my amazement, and Mother's, it was plucked from a slush pile and accepted for publication. When I met with the editor, she regarded me a long time before saying, "If half of this shit happened, lord help you." A couple of weeks after it came out I got a call from her saying she had received a letter from Mother.

"Really? What does she say?"

"Should I read it to you?"

"Yeah. Might as well."

I am very proud of my daughter Augusta's first published story, a craft she learned from me, though, I found the mother rather a pale character. If she wanted a full-fledged portrait, the mother would have been far bitchier and, although I do understand it might not have fit in with the themes of the story, I think it would have helped if some of my columns had been included. Still, as I said, for a first effort, I am deeply proud.

Sincerely, Mab Quick.

The editor could not understand my laughter, nor would she agree to publish it in the letters to the editor. I was as disappointed as Mother.

Why do the scales have to fall from our eyes? Why couldn't I still be in the thrall of that woman, think her unmanageable and unimaginable personality just a lot of fun? She once wore a plastic cheese-dish top as a hat to a party, for god's sake. Why couldn't I hold on to that and leave the rest to rot?

I think I have straightened out Frances. Of course, now all the other pictures look crooked so I've come into the bedroom to give my eyes a break. Lena is in here. I can't have her on the wall. Superstition. I can't have her where my eye might fall on her, so she's in the closet, top shelf, an unseen shrine. It's her school portrait, so everything has been airbrushed out, not that she had many flaws. I remember the day; Lena, Heather, Leslie and I all found ourselves waiting at the same time to be shuttled before the camera. Billy Underhill made some snide remark about a sister act. But he knew well enough that Heather and Leslie weren't my sisters, only Lena's.

I was surprised that it was this school photo of her by my father's bed. He took so many of her. Perhaps, he wanted it close because it was the same one he gave to the various private detectives he hired to try and find her. Or, maybe he liked that she is looking into the middle distance. I like that too. As I pull out a skirt, or a blouse, there she is staring over the top of my head, indifferent to my sartorial choices.

I can hear the first of the buses rumbling by. The nightly exodus has begun. C thinks I'm crazy, but I sometimes suspect that the legions of construction workers, those poor souls from Pakistan and god knows where else, all wearing the same colour jumpsuit being ferried by the thousands back to what I can only imagine are shit-hole workers' camps, don't just stare at me as I am walking the dogs because I'm a woman but rather because I am a phenomenon. The human brain is wired, after all, to suck up information. Curiosity for Christ's sake. What the fuck do they have to look at except each other and another slab of concrete being added to this rising skyline? From my balcony alone, I look out over five major construction sites.

"No, they want to fuck you."

He's probably right. But unlike a hot-blooded New York construction worker, his wolf whistle raining down on you like bullets, five hundred men staring at you deletes the un-nerve. Perhaps, next time I'm out walking the dogs, I should flash my tits. Haven't done that in a while. Used to show my tits all the time. Frances too. Though I imagine she has kept her's under wraps for years now. I wonder what Lena would have made of me, of Frances. I found among my father's things letters he wrote to her, with nowhere to send, trying to describe us.

"Frances seems to have settled in LA. It's not a city that I would imagine suits, but on our rare phone calls, she is quite adamant that she is happy. Too adamant?"

"Augati has recently married an up and coming writer. Though in my mind she's still a child, one who has spilled a bottle of honey on the floor and turned it into flypaper trying to clean it up. Thank god, it was a Friday, and you arrived soon after and could help."

What a weird thing to try to describe your grown-up children to a missing daughter. No wonder he fell back onto a childhood memory.

I do remember spilling the honey. No matter what I did, it just smeared more.

And, I did marry, at a young age, an up and coming writer. Not C. Marcelo. When I told him about finding my father's letters to Lena, he said he was definitely going to use that in a story.

One of C's colleagues has asked if he can interview me, the ex-wife of such a well known Latin American writer. Marcelo and I have been friends so long now it is near inconceivable that we were once married. But he was the one who took this little rat, burrowing in grief and madness, lost in a big city, showing her tits hither and yon, and pulled me out by the tail, let me sniff real air, made me look around and see that there was a whole world who didn't give a shit that my sister was nearly murdered and had disappeared, didn't give a shit that my family had fractured, didn't give a shit, unless I made something of it, turned it into, dare I say art? I didn't, of course. Never had the balls. But that didn't matter. It was a step out. My first brush with love and what turned out to be an abiding friendship.

He got a real kick out of my latest piece for Salon magazine about watching porn in a Muslim country which is impossible unless you have a VPN provider. My hands and mind may be typing in Abu Dhabi, but the brains of my computer thinks it's in Frankfurt. I'm not that big a porn watcher and found I was more interested in the German ads. There's a lot for butter. That can't be happenstance, can it? Marcelo texted me as soon as he read it.

Tell me more.

So I told him about the fat Ozzies who haunt the bars where young Asian women dressed up as Catholic school girls have to endure meaty paws on their slender thighs. They have to endure more than that, but I'm witness to only the opening notes of this dispiriting ritual.

It's all so creepy, and I have to admit all this repressed shit is having an effect on my own desires.

These men still being ferried past in buses, what hope do they have? You see them on Friday nights filling the streets of Abu Dhabi. There's one mall in particular with a few craggy trees in front where the workers congregate on bare patches of grass. On those nights, in order to get to the entrance, you have to wade through them as one would a sea of ducks, the same slow paddle to let you pass. I sometimes wonder if the humidity pushed into the Gulf by India's monsoon winds is their revenge, except, they are the ones who have to toil in the soupy brown heat, unthinkable once to a Canadian like me, and still perceived as un-livable. Lately, though, we've had some strange rains, downpours that sent the gutters sputtering and spewing back the deluge causing the roads to flood.

I was thrilled until I found out that the clouds had been seeded which made grotesque the rumbles of thunder and the heavy drops of rain beating down on a desert already under the assault of an urban onslaught. And, if the powers that be can take a frail little cloud and turn it into a tempest, I wouldn't be surprised if they added a dash of saltpetre. More than a million horny men must be a worry.

Sex and weather. Fifteen times a day, I must walk to this sliding door that leads to my balcony and the Gulf beyond to look at the cloudless sky and try and read the weather. I'm getting better at finding subtle clues on the waves. But I take most comfort in the windsock down below. There are windsocks all over the place here. A remnant of the days when this was a featureless expanse and minute shifts of sand grains were not enough of a visual for any pilot. I think I'm going to cry. I love those windsocks, so elemental, the one thing that doesn't seem a hologram.

I can see now the tail end of the caravan of buses, it usually takes more than an hour to ferry the workers out, and when they are gone, there will be a palpable relief among my neighbours. Nobody likes to be reminded on whose backs all this splendour rests.

C will be home soon. I should turn some lights on. He hates coming back to a dark house. And, put a beer in the freezer, so it's ice cold.

W hat I wouldn't give to see a mouse dropping. Sitting in this bar, surrounded by marble and plushness, and all I want is to be standing in our collapse cabin, avoiding a bat swooping around my head. Never thought I'd be saying this. When my parents buy that wild thorny patch of land in the Eastern Townships about an hour's drive from Montreal, I am not so keen on it. The log cabin is such a wreck that it is thrown in for free. It smells dank and mean. And, is always cold. But my father revels in the hand-hued beams and solid plank floors and manages to ignore that there is no running water, or a bathroom, or, for much of my youth, electricity. In the beginning, every weekend is devoted to tearing down walls insulated with old newspaper, sweeping out mounds of porcupine shit, battling bats, screaming at wandering snakes, dealing with cobwebs, pulling out endless splinters, and because of all the protruding rusty nails, I am continually getting tetanus boosters.

Into this mayhem, every other weekend, Lena arrives. What amazes me is she doesn't seem to mind leaving what I think must be the height of luxury, her mother and step-father's country cottage a mere five miles down the road. Not mind leaving Heather, who is so beautiful that I feel like a slug beside her, or Leslie who is, cruelly, a mess: a cross-eye, knock knees, strangely sloping shoulders. Their vast physical difference explained and accepted because they are both adopted. Not mind leaving a cottage on a lake with a bathroom, two in fact. A sailing boat. And, a roof that doesn't leak and a lawn that isn't weed-choked. Though all of this information is on hearsay since I am not allowed anywhere near the place. Not mind leaving her mother with her "gardening clothes"—a broad-brimmed hat, overalls, and work gloves to hold her dainty trowel—her step-father off to play golf and her sisters, doing what I imagine must be the coolest things in the world. Leave all that to stay with us where we have to brush mouse droppings off the table before we can sit down to eat. Where no sleep is to be had because of the racket the porcupines make hell-bent on reclaiming what had long been their private domain. They succeed in the end. The cabin, having been wholly eaten on one side, has collapsed.

In my suspicious little mind, I figure the only reason Lena is willing to give up clean sheets and a working TV, give up two parents that aren't at each other's throats is because she is Daddy's favourite. (How little I knew or saw) How else to explain her eagerness? I watch with deep resentment as she and my father launch into some ambitious project together like gouging out a hiking trail so one can take contemplative walks through the woods. They never manage to do much about the deer and black flies or the mosquitoes. How else to explain why she is willing to act the air traffic controller, making sure my father's path is clear as he performs the unenviable task of hauling out from the dark, cobweb-ridden corner the poo bucket we use in winter when going to the outhouse is not feasible. Mother and I stand way back, though the smell, in the warm, stove-heated cabin, is not so easily escaped so I walk around with a scarf covering my mouth, pretending to retch until my father cuffs the back of my head.

Lena never annoys my father. Ceding to the fact that

memory is mostly in lock-down and new ones rarely ferreted out, try as I might, I can't remember my father, whose violence is corporal in nature, with the odd ramped up alcohol-fuelled rage, ever hitting Lena. She did, however, like to point out a that if he keeps bashing me about the head, he might cause brain damage.

My mother doesn't fare much better. It infuriates him that she is constantly setting her sleeves on fire while cooking on the wood-stove. And in truth, hair-raising are the weekends when Lena isn't there, and Mother offers to help my father with whatever project he has going. Nothing worse than an incompetent holding a spanner or trying to guess if something is level. "For fuck's sake, Mab, is it straight?" My mother, terrified, calls me over and even with the two of us considering every angle, pitched up against a world of uneven floorboards, warped rafters, and undulating land, the question is impossible to answer. I wonder now if that's the reason I feel less than confident when hanging pictures? But really how much can you blame on your parents? Everything?

What would Lena make of all this marble? She liked rocks, like them before I did. There were times when Mother, fed up with trying to keep the wood-stove lit, or swatting away flies as she made dinner, insisted that we drive into the States, which is only ten miles away, to have dinner and see a drive-in movie. Off we'd go, my father in a temper, through the long summer evening, crossing at a small town called Beebe where most of the houses are made from granite. Lena is the one who points that out to me, tells me there is a pit nearby, a famous granite pit. I remember thinking too bad the town isn't near a diamond mine or a marble quarry. The granite houses look small and cold, grey and lonely. Sitting in this marble mausoleum those sad little houses now seem sweet, or at least, built to a human scale. I can't help but wonder which of the new hotels being built along this coastline is going to be the one that causes Italy to collapse because the marble that used to hold it up has been shipped here so that fat Germans, wealthy Arabs, squawking Brits with their families and every other bored pleasure seeker can feel they are in the lap of luxury and having a high old time. If France is going to be raped of its sand and Italy its marble can't they at least come up with something less god awful? This drink, however, is nice.

And yes, I'll have another.

Does Lena still like rocks? She was/is a natural scientist, not by training, or maybe by training, who knows, but she is the one who, when I excitedly find a huge boulder hidden deep in the woods and name it "Augati's Rock", who tells me that it was dropped there by the receding ice age. If I looked closer, she says, I can see how the rock was scarred as it was dragged along until the ice let it go and there it sat for thousands of years until I came along and named it.

This marble, if I narrow in, is not just the slick facade for the nouveau riche but something the earth wrought with history in its veins. I have noticed there's no white marble. Perhaps Michelangelo and the other masters used it all up. I hope so.

There, faintly, the call to prayer. It never fails to move me. There were bells from the scores of Catholic churches wafting across Montreal on Sundays. If I hadn't been so bored, I might have thought it rather lovely. Hearing the call to prayer does add an exotic note to this shopping mall. I have been warned to keep my godlessness under wraps. Having no god is worse than being an infidel. And not having children? Oh boy.

It must be damn confusing to be a Muslim kid these days. The malls are groaning with Christmas decorations, Santas, angels, the whole bit. I was in Ace hardware the other day. Christmas carols and hymns serenaded us as fake snow swirled through the air. There were Christmas trees dressed to the nines, and scores of miniature alpine villages replete with skaters spinning on mirrored ice. An Emirati woman fought to pull her son along. He was dazzled by the displays and enraged that he wasn't being plied with all this crap. I felt sorry for her. When I was a kid acting up in the store, it was the low threats of bodily harm issued from pursed lips that worked to keep me in check. But this woman was veiled. What her lips or eyes were doing was a mystery. The boy, in full melt-down, wasn't to be mollified, not even when, pitched to drown out "Silent Night," the call to prayer sounded. My editor at the online magazine thought that would make a good story, but I'm not up to working at the moment. Maybe in the New Year, I'll write one called. "I'm godless. I'm childless. I'm fucked."

My next drink. And the attendant rigmarole. Yes, the first one was lovely, Yes, this one looks perfect too. No, I don't need any more chips. Yes, my husband will be joining me. No, don't bring his beer yet, he likes it cold. Yes, it is a pleasant evening.

I wonder what is keeping C. He most likely ran into a

colleague. At times it feels like everyone at the university is connected to one another on a concentric conveyor belt. Pass once, pass twice. Hello. Hello.

Happy Hour is over, and most of the other drinkers have cleared off, and I am alone. I am alone with my musings of marble and memories of paths hacked, of sleeves aflame, of poo buckets and of mice droppings, of Christmas carols being drowned out by the call to prayer, and a slight Muslim boy who would love nothing more than to have tinsel in his hair. I am alone needing new thoughts, so I turn towards the night and wonder what this land was like when it was still empty, though not to the Bedouin. I would have liked to sail on a dhow on the sea now inky black and unseen.

But second by second I am losing the battle. It is today. It is this week. Now. And, no matter how much I coach myself not to fall prey to it, not to brood over or churn up the horror, I am limp, I am helpless. The nights will be bad, the days will be bad, the hours, the solitude and, the conversations meant to soothe will all be bad as I am marched forward right up to the moment Leslie was axed to death. Lena maimed for life. And, Frances nearly died in the snow.

We came home last night to find that the air conditioning was on the fritz. And, then we made the fatal error of opening the balcony doors which flooded the apartment with milky heat. There's a man now in my kitchen pulling down panels from the ceiling checking some duct or another with what sounds like a Geiger counter, which is a bit worrisome. I have things on the stove, kale, and I'm cooking down white beans in a broth. A strange man by my stove is upsetting.

I don't know what to do with myself. I can't very well work. Not that I have the energy.

The air thick, C and I couldn't sleep. We lay on top of the bed, the dogs choosing to stay on the stone floor. The Times had called and wants him to do a story on elephants in South Africa who have been raping rhinos. If he does it, he'll have to leave soon to go do research. "Humans acting crazy, that's one thing. But animals," he sighed. We were silent for a bit then C turned to me and asked when I first knew that Heather was a psycho.

"The library book," I told him.

He nodded. "I always thought you should write a story about that day."

"I don't know."

"Tell it to me, tell me the whole thing. It might help to see your way forward."

"But you know it."

"I don't care."

"If I were to write it I would start with me, seven years old, standing on a filthy, ice-encrusted snow mound, one of the many mini-mountains created by snow ploughs

23

and always the last to melt come spring. My jacket open, my winter mittens long lost, my boots, though still needed, heavy on my feet. I have an audience, four or five neighbourhood kids, and I'm trying to explain the nature of my family.

'I have my Dad,' I say. 'But before he was my Dad, he was married to someone else. And they had a baby. My sister Lena. But then he fell in love with my mum, and Lena's mum fell in love with my father's business partner.'

'That's not allowed,' one kid says.

'Yeah, that's not allowed,' chimes in another.

'It is,' I tell them, 'if it's like a swap. Everybody swaps. So my dad came to Mum. And Liv went to Piers.'

'What happened to the baby?'

'Nothing happened to her. She's my sister. But, not a whole. A half. So she doesn't live with us except on weekends.'

'Is that why she's half,' another kid asks. 'because she doesn't live with you?'

'No! My mum isn't her mum. Her mum is her mum and the mum to Lena's other sisters Heather and Leslie. But they are not whole or half; they are adopted.'

'But if they are your sister sisters how come, they aren't yours?'

I stamp my foot. 'Because they are adopted! And not by my dad but by Lena's stepdad. Liv and Piers went up to Newfoundland and got them and brought them back to be sisters to Lena.'

'Got them from who?'

'From nuns.'

This confuses them. Nuns and children? Not the usual mix.

'Why not just have a baby?' someone asks.

On my mound, I pause. I know the words that explains the reason but not the meaning. 'Liv,' I say, 'lost her womb.'"

While giving birth to Lena something had gone horribly wrong, but I've never been clear on what it was, but as a result, she was infertile. Piers never forgave my father. It, somehow, being his fault.

C shifted. I don't think even now he can follow the line of siblings, half, adopted, or step-parents, who was screwing who, when and where. But I told him many times despite the swap and the hostility between the former business partners, Mother and Liv were quite friendly. We lived ten blocks apart so it wasn't uncommon that they would run into each other in the supermarket. Liv's cart was a thing of beauty. She had all like-minded items ranged together so when rung up by the cashier the receipt had meat, fish, vegetables and household goods all itemized together and clear for Piers' to review. Such order flipped Mother out. Whenever she saw her cart she'd start babbling, 'Oh, my filthy flat and unshaved legs, ignore my ink-stained fingers, and no, I have no idea what I'm going to make for dinner, something slapdash!' Meanwhile, Liv wore a cool look of sympathy without getting any of the humour of it. Yet, there was a bond. Perhaps all women, if they allow themselves, feel some sisterhood with the other woman.

"What I don't know," I continued, "as I stand on my ice mound, never quite succeeding in making clear our convoluted family, is that it's about to get bigger. Mother is pregnant. Something, as you know, she doesn't become aware of until she is nearly in her sixth month. Then it is, as they say, a shock. Especially for my father, who is deep in the planning stages of running off with his mistress."

"You never told me that?"

"Yeah, some French woman. He can barely contain his rage in the weeks before the birth as he slaps up wallpaper to ready the baby's room. Even Lena, when she is on hand to help, can't calm him down. Frances will spend much of her early months being rescued from beneath peeling sheets of rosebud wallpaper lying limply across her cot.

But you know what I want more than anything that afternoon? I want my audience to understand, that while Lena and I may have different mothers, we are sisters. I have no other. Once I know Mother is pregnant, I worry what having a whole sister will mean and, that feels like such a betrayal. Lena, who shares no blood with Heather and Leslie, has never expressed any ambivalence about her feelings towards her adopted sisters. If anything, I am the other. The one who stands alone. But now there is going to be a baby to which Lena, blood-wise, will only have half-claim."

"Madam? Madam?"

Oh, I'm being called.

Never before a Madam. The maintenance man has found a flaw, a kink in the duct, something. He's explaining the problem as we walk from room to room. Big job. That I get. How long? Today done. That I get too. But more men needed and different tools. For all the seeming luxury I find myself in, this building is more like a funhouse than a solid bulwark against the heat and dust. The lights in the hallways flicker on and off. Sometimes standing outside waiting for the dogs to pee, I watch an arbitrary light show as various hallways blaze and then dip into darkness. Alarms go off all the time, and the elevator often lurches to a stop, sighs and then starts up again.

The man wants me to sign a release form. What I'm releasing I have no clue, just as I have no idea how he'll get paid. I've never lived so detached from my utilities. Bills can't be sent. To where? We have no mailbox or address. Somewhere there exists a P.O. box that has been designated, but we haven't been able to fathom where it is. Thank God for the university. C, at least, managed to figure out his P.O. box there.

Anyhow, he's gone now to get more men. I should have my lunch. Although, just as I'm about to take my first bite, no doubt the bell will ring.

The beans are still hard. The kale is done. I stare into the fridge, but nothing is springing to mind. C and I ate the lasagna. You wouldn't think in the heat we'd get hungry, but last night we found ourselves peckish so I brought into the bedroom the last of the lasagna, C picking at the crispy bits while I continued my story.

"On the walk home after holding court on my snow mount, I am half enraged that my friends are so dull-witted and half pleased that my family is like no other.

The outside stairs still have ice on them, but there must have been a succession of warm days because the storm windows have been removed and I notice once inside how much lighter the flat feels, and the street sounds are no longer muffled.

To my 'I'm home.' Mother replies, 'I can't stop.'

It never changes. Never Varies. No 'I'm busy.' No 'Give me a sec.'

That closed door: me on the outside, her on the inside with whatever it is she can't stop: writing her column, or pounding out her broadcast, or in a panic about her T.V. show. But I never ask her to stop. I don't want her to. I like that she is on one side of the door and I the other.

"You still do," C said.

I nodded. "It is funny how I never think of her, never see her sitting in Frances' backroom, words mostly gone, eyes gone, hands gone, life as she knew it, as we knew it, gone. Then I'll be chopping a carrot, and I am swamped by her."

C took up my hand and then dropped it. You need ac in AD if you have any desire to be tactile.

"Her door closed, I go into the kitchen to heat some baked beans for my afternoon snack. When I am finished, I take the pot with its few unfinished beans and go stand by the back balcony so I can stare down at the street. Westmount always had a stillness about it, so when a neighbour came into view, it was slightly unbelievable, as if they were play-acting walking their dogs or taking in the groceries. But on that day it isn't a neighbour that appears on stage but Lena. I am so taken aback that I instantly shrink from view.

It is a Tuesday and a school night. The rules of her other house—always a source of fascination, mainly because there are no rules at mine—are such that there is no wandering the streets of Westmount at four in the afternoon on a Tuesday. That is homework time. Followed by bath time, topped with mealtime, then after clearing the dishes, reading time, and if all had been executed properly then perhaps an hour of television. The power of these rules is so strong that when Lena comes to us for the weekend rather than maintaining our usual slothful ways, we find ourselves forced into lockstep. It drives my mother crazy, but even she can't fight it. It is a possessed woman, who, after dinner, under Lena's steady-state stare, claps her hands and says. 'Right girls, dishes, reading, and then a spot of T.V.'

From the shadows, I watch as Lena, her book bag strapped across her chest, her head down, never once looking up to our flat, walks along the block toward us and then out of view. A minute later, the doorbell rings. I creep down the hallway and tap on mother's door and wait until I hear her stop typing.

'I think there's someone at the door,' I say.

'Well, answer it.'

'I think it might be Lena.'

A palpable annoyance radiates from behind the door until an abrupt, 'She's your bloody sister.'

Boy, that stung. Yes, every other weekend Lena came over, moved the clothes in my chest-of-drawers to one side, laid out her pressed, clean, unstained, hand-sewn shirts and pants that smelled like they had been washed in lavender. And at night we shared a bed like we shared a father. But the fantasy of sisterly-ness was never quite reached. It bugged me. And it bugged me more that it didn't seem to bug her. She was there because she was Miles Quick's daughter. If he had lived elsewhere or had a different second wife and a different second daughter... I always felt an imposter sister."

"That's ridiculous." C said.

"Maybe. But that's how I felt."

I reached down and found my sweating beer on the floor, took a swig, then picked up the story again.

"I hesitate on the top step. Mother resumes her typing, but I can tell she is merely pounding out letters. Real words don't have a rhythm.

Lena certainly seems her outwardly placid self while waiting for me to come down the stairs and open the front door, which she knows is rarely locked. It is only once I open the door that I see she is crying. Small neat tears."

C couldn't believe it.

"No snot? No Ubangi lips? No swollen-shut eyes? Christ, when you cry, you look a fucking wreck."

It's true. Twelve rounds at least.

"No, Lena's tears are lovely. And, rarely seen. I am so shocked that for the longest time, I just stand there staring at her until she finally asks if she can come in. But when I tell her that Daddy is in England buying cars, the two of us are completely stumped. Finally, she says maybe she should speak to Mum. We climb the stairs and wait outside Mab's door until the sheer weight of our unseen presence is enough that she has no choice but to get up.

'What the hell is going on?' she says, opening her door.

'I've run away.'

'From where?'

'My home.'

'That's not possible.'

I have to agree with Mum here. What Lena is saying makes no sense. Running away requires a revolt of some kind and the only person from Lena's other home who is even remotely capable of that kind of action is Heather. Both mother and I know that. But here is Lena, head bowed, looking a bit lost, telling us she has run away from home.

'Why?'

'Heather violated my library book.'

'Violated?" Mother raises an eyebrow.

'She stenciled in stuff all over the pages.'

'Stenciled?'

'Yes. So it isn't in her handwriting. So she can say it wasn't her and there will be no way of proving if it is.'

Mother is thoroughly intrigued now.

'What on earth did she write?"

'Lots of things.'

'Oh, come on, Lena.'

I, wanting to help, say, 'Piss?'

'No, not that. She wrote: The Queen can suck Québécois cock. And, other stuff.'

Mother bursts out laughing, 'As she bloody well should. Sounds to me like Heather has improved your library book considerably.'

I, on the other hand, don't see what is so funny. 'Lena will get blamed,' I say. 'She took the book out.'

Mother gives me a long stare then turns to Lena, 'Your father is in England buying cars. And I can't stop. You, girls, do what you need to do.'"

Damn the doorbell. The ac man is back with two other men They have ladders, and piping, toolboxes, and they want to start in the kitchen. I should have found something in the fridge. I am starving. But they have an important job, and my sighs and general agitation aren't helping matters. But there's nothing to be done; I can't sit still. Never could.

People always compared Lena and me. Her still. Me not. But they were wrong. All you had to do was hold her hand, feel the energy, and the tremendous effort expended to keep it all in check to understand that while I may have been perpetually bopping around, she was a fucking volcano. Not that she ever blew. Or maybe she did once, and that's what saved her. I liked to think that.

I just realised the lasagna pan is still on the floor. I can't have these maintenance men seeing it. What would they think? How decadent are our lives that we eat pasta in bed? But I can't bring it into the kitchen. Maybe they won't see it.

And, I think the dogs licked it clean. Unlike Lena, who pushed aside the plate of beans on toast I had made. I don't blame her; in my haste, I barely heated them and then ripped the bread trying to give her a treat of extra butter.

I must have dipped in my narrative at that point because I felt C give me a nudge. "What happened after your mother closed the door?"

"What happens? I tell Lena that she has no choice but to live with us. I have this nagging conviction that the intrinsic missing link to our sisterhood will be bridged if we live together full time. Ignoring her protestations that she has homework to do, I drag her into my bedroom where I knock half my books onto the floor, dump out my bottom drawer of all its pill-y sweaters and jeans, toss everything out from my closet. When I turn around show

Lena just how much space there is, she isn't there. I find her in the dining room brushing off the crumbs from the Indian bedspread tablecloth so she can lay out her school books.

'Does Heather really want the Queen to suck Quebecois cock?'

'I don't know.'

'I bet she does and it's because of the war.'

'I doubt it.'

'But that doesn't make sense. Because we love the Queen and Heather isn't French. Though maybe before she was adopted, she had some French blood, and it's showing up now.'

'I don't think she has French blood.'

'How do you know?'

'I don't but...'

'You mean because she kinda looks Chinese?'

'She's not Chinese.'

'How do you know?'

'She's not Chinese,' Lena says, "And, she's not French."

'But she wants the Queen to suck...,' I persist.

'She just wanted to ruin my library book. That's all.'

'Bet she was glad though they blew up the Queen in the post office?'

Not two weeks before at our local Post Office, a homemade bomb had gone off. Since then, rumours have been flying.

'They didn't blow up the Queen, only her picture.'

'I know that, but someone got mangled.'

'That's not true. Just the picture got ruined.'

'No blood on the wall?'

'Not even a burn mark.'

I hate that Lena is throwing dirt on all the rumours. She is such a killjoy. 'How do you know.' I ask.

'We went and posted letters. Piers wanted to show that we weren't afraid of the Separatists and their dirty tricks.'

'Did Heather post a letter?'

'I guess.'

'Then I bet she wrote one to the French telling them that they should try again. And kill someone this time.'"

"You said that?" C looked at me. Was this part of my story, or the story?

"I did."

"Fuck."

"I was seven! I didn't know Heather was going to become a psycho killer. You know it just occurs to me that Lena must have known something, intuited something, because she abruptly stood up and said she was going to be sick. A moment later, I hear the bathroom door lock. I am in shock. I don't think I have ever announced I was going to be sick. It's preposterous, an undermining of the calamity that is throwing up. And, I am certainly not going to deal with this on my own. Once again, Mother is forced to stop working.

'What?'

'Lena is being sick.'

'What did you do?'

'Nothing!'

A pause and then the scrape of her chair. I try not to look guilty when the door opens. I am, after all, blameless. But a sick stepdaughter is worrying. My father will no doubt catch wind of the whole thing and how mother responded. I think when my mother began what was admittedly a torrid affair with my father she never took into consideration what it would mean to be a stepmother."

"Does anyone?" C wondered.

"Now, I suppose. The whole blended family bullshit. Divorced parents being best friends."

"You have to include how they meet in the story."

"I do, don't I? They meet at the newspaper. Miles has started writing a weekend column about the history of some of his vintage vehicles. History, humour and his infectious passion for cars even has mother glancing at his byline. But it isn't until there is a threat of a strike among the printers that she actually sees him. Well, hears him. My father, forever trying to figure out how to scam the inevitability of decay, has screwed taps into his shoes so his heels and soles last forever. While the writers and editors gather in serious knots trying to decide how best to support the printers while not letting their own financial lives go to wrack and ruin, my father can be heard tip-tapping down the hall. He spies mother right off. In the inevitable repairing to a bar after the meeting, two people did what only two people madly attracted to each other can do, create an illusion, and shape-shift, finding that their shadow selves fit perfectly, while their corporeal bodies stood by sensing a future disaster. But then, none of it matters.

It should have just been a few fucks, before a cooling down and return to previous lives, after all, Miles had Lena at home. But..."

"Oh, is this where the famous switch happens."

"Pretty soon. Daddy isn't the only one fucking around.

Liv is having it off with Piers. My father is outraged. His business partner? And truly, since my father knows vintage cars but not how to sell them. Piers understands their value but not how to love them.

With Liv in love with Piers my mother becomes a lifeline. He turns up the charm while tamping down the baby daughter, his love for her and his guilt over leaving her. Mother, blind in love, sees none of this. Before the year is out, just as they are starting to see that a center made of sex might not hold, she is pregnant with me. A new family is born. But mother, as the logic of their love grows more suspect, can never quite forget that Liv had left Miles first and Lena, the hapless victim, the most favoured child, brings out her worst instincts; she is jealous as shit of her. Which, in turn, churns up all her insecurities. Lena comes from the stablest of stable homes, is always so neat and tidy, right down, or up, to her heavy glossy hair never falling out of its ponytail. Never, let's face it, like mine. Rats tails rather than pigtails. Mother feels all of this keenly. So as the lock sounds on the bathroom door she wants to make damn sure that I understand that Lena's throwing up is my fault. After all, I had fed her the beans.

'Darling, are you alright?' Mother asks laying a hand on Lena's brow.

'Yes, but I couldn't brush my teeth.'

'Oh dear. Why not?'

Lena shrugs, 'I don't have a toothbrush.'

So what does mother do? Offers mine! And, when I start to freak out, she tells me not to be a pill. Lena, a little weak, goes and sits on the couch.

'I'll just wait,' she says.

Mother and I look at each other. Wait for what? Daddy won't be back from England for another week. Or, is she waiting for mother, or me, to go out and buy her a toothbrush? It is always hard to tell with Lena what she is thinking.

'Does Liv know you're here?'

God knows what got into me, but I rush at mother nearly pushing her over. 'She ran away! She needs to live here!'

Before Mother can swat me aside, Lena says, 'Call mum'.

"No! Lena! Stay here!"

I was, and am, a bit surprised how much I wanted her to stay. Lena, on the other hand, looked miserable. I think of her now, ten years old, needing to run away and having only the unpalatable choice of our house, foreign without my father. Real escape, when it finally did present itself, must have seemed a dream. No wonder she took it. Damn the rest of us."

C took up my hand again, our palms instantly springing with sweat.

"She looks so small sitting on the couch waiting for her mother to come. Heather, the defaced library book, Lena running away and her throwing up, none of it was mentioned. Liv just says she'll be right over.

She arrives, a little breathless, wearing kid gloves, a Herringbone coat cinched tightly around her slim waist and her boots with not a trace of salt stains. Someone else's mother? Your sister's mother? Fuck. My father had loved her! I look at Mab, who, as usual, is in her writing clothes, draw-string Indian pants and an old cardigan which she holds tightly around her body.

I wait. Is anyone going to mention the fact that Heather had stenciled, what Liv would call "naughty language" into a library book? Apparently not. Liv and mother start talking about Leslie's eyes, or to be precise, about one of them, which even after two operations, still roves over to one corner. Liv keeps looking over at me. Leslie and I are the same age, in a different life, we might be friends. Though, to my shame, I would never have been friends with such a physical wreck, although, I did sense, that at some point, Leslie might be the conduit into the Driscoll household, and in the end, she is, if only for a moment.

I wonder if the two mothers will go on chatting forever when Liv finally says that they must go. Piers likes to have his dinner on the table precisely at seven. Mother has her hand on my shoulder, a grip that communicates acutely that I am not, now that this unlikely episode is about to come to a merciful close, to open my mouth, not for any reason, but certainly not to mention the library book or what Heather had done.

Lena and Liv work their way down the inside stairs through a slalom course of boots, skates and cross-country skis, errant gloves, mittens and scarves. Mother and I go over to the window, before they come into view we hear Lena tell her mother that she should hang onto the bannister. As Lena gets into the car, we can see in the front seat the shadowed outline of Heather; her knees pressed up against the dashboard."

"Jesus."

"When I turn away from the window, I am alone. Mother has gone back into her office. Time. I had no clue what to do with it."

38

"More beans on toast?"
"Probably."

Aircon fixed. And, I'm fucking freezing. There was C stumbling around in the middle of the night, trying to regulate the blast of air buffeting us. Naturally, this morning it's cloudy and cool. Real clouds. It's so overcast that I didn't even bother to take my sunglasses when I walked the dogs. I ran into everyone I knew in the complex. They weren't wearing sunglasses either. Eyes! Eye contact. What a surprise. We, Westerners, are the reverse image of covered women. They are all eyes, no body. While we are no eyes, all body. Until today that is. To suddenly have eyes trained on me was a bit unnerving. I had to fight the urge to say, "Shit, you look like that!? I would never have suspected."

It has also undercut my long-held assumption that I have a pretty good idea what an Emirati woman looks like even if she's completely covered. One does become a bit of a reader-of-the-veils, sort of like the way I read my windsock, looking for subtle clues of the woman beneath the folds of black and greedily noting any flash of colour as they walk on by. You know they are just chafing at the bit. Even in the short time I've been here, I've noticed that their abayas have begun sporting more designs: rhinestone studs, gold piping, fringed hems. I do like, however, how proud the fully-veiled women are. I suppose completely hidden; they can strut their stuff.

C says I remind him of the Terminator when I look at women. The rapid calculation, stem to stern. But I'm not judging. I'm searching. Weirdly, since arriving here, I have been consumed by this perverse fantasy that Lena, having found solace in a covered life, is walking past me, her eyes incurious, her hands tucked away. But the truth is that half these women, their beauty undeniable even when shrouded, remind me more of Heather; dark, regal, exacting. That was always the greatest surprise, that junkyard child, moving as though possessed by eons of rarified airs.

I am, by far, the scruffiest of the dog walkers. I tried when we first arrived to clean up my act. Dabbed kohl around my eyes, fished out earrings, but all that fell away. I can't compete with these women, decked out in their yoga pants and neon running shoes, though now I've seen their eyes, I know what an effort it all is. Today we commented on the weather, how lovely, how Christmas-y, how we hope it lasts the week so we can pretend, come Christmas morn, that we're not in the desert.

As we chatted, were they reading anything in my eyes? Am I a dead give away? I've looked in the mirror often enough trying to see, stared right through the cornea, peering, peering, to the fabled seat of the soul. It all must be there, but where, where?

When we were kids sometimes Lena and I would get locked into impromptu staring contests: the first to look away, loses. I couldn't stand it, fearing no recognition. But I always fought to win. Until, one afternoon, I caught her eye, held her gaze only to have her get up and lock herself in the bathroom. It was only later that I found out that she had awakened in the night to find Heather standing over her just staring. Even in the gloaming, Lena knew everything depended on her not turning away.

Poor Lena, with all her secrets, her shaded life, just dark enough that I couldn't read the clues; neither could anyone else for that matter.

These clouds, I'm thinking, look awfully suspicious. Too heavy. But I can't hear any buzzing planes if that's how you seed clouds.

Frances?

Skyping me? It's nearly eleven at night in LA. She's drunk, of course. But fair is fair. She is ordering me to sit still but I want her to see the clouds.

"Fuck the clouds."

"But do they seem fake?"

She tries to straighten her glasses. One of her dogs ate the arm. It was the last standing pair.

"Why are you awake?" I ask.

Frances knocks her hand on her head. Why staying up late requires one of her myriad rituals, I don't know. Perhaps the change is upsetting. Both she and C arm themselves with all manner of tics: checking the stove, keeping knives in separate drawers, taking things said back three times, never leaving one shoe at an awkward angle to its mate and on and on. The fates, I tell them, don't care, but I shouldn't; armour is armour.

Frances is looking down; is she crying?

"I had a dream about Lena."

"The usual one?"

"I wish. Hold on."

I watch the screen as Frances disappears, leaving me with a view of her kitchen. It and I are expectant, hearing the ghostly satellite distortions as she blows her nose in the bathroom. Her usual dream is that she and Lena are putting band-aids over her Barbie doll's tits to cover up the holes Frances had created with a pin. Entering the kitchen again, she stops to pour herself another drink.

She sits back down. She's not collected at all, and her nose is still running.

"What was last night's dream?"

"It was new, but it felt old as I was dreaming it."

"Maybe you had it before but didn't remember?"

Frances considers this.

"I was trying to get onto Lena's bed."

"Which bed?"

She gives me a look. There's only one bed.

"Sorry."

"I'm climbing and climbing, but there are too many tubes and things in the way. So I give up. And, as soon as I do, I feel very good. Happy even."

"I like that dream."

"You don't think it's cruel?"

"One person in this family should be un-haunted."

"How can I be un-haunted with you around?"

She starts crying again.

"Do you have any cucumbers?" I ask.

Frances turns and looks at her fridge. "No, mother ate the last of them. Why?"

"For your eyes."

"They were Persian. You know how we get? I'd need fifteen slices just for my bags alone."

Getting up, Frances pours herself another drink

"I met a bunch of women today for the first time without their sunglasses," I tell her. "They looked nothing like I thought they would."

"That happens all the time in LA. You gotta learn to judge by lips."

"Remember how mother, with lips so pursed they were

nearly white, would try and keep us in check with her steady stream of threats?"

"You more than me."

"Wonder what she would have done if she was a Muslim woman with her face covered?"

"Probably just hit us outright. You see any women bashing on their kids?"

"Nah, never. Which is probably why they are such brats. Even if their mothers' lips are white with rage, how the hell would they know?"

"Oh my god!" Frances falls forward slightly and has to grip the counter. "In my dream, Lena had her eyes taped shut."

I have to pause. That time. It is more of a dream for Frances, not an imprint. She was, after all, only six.

"They were taped shut," I say.

"They were?"

"She was in a coma."

"So why then tape her eyes?"

I don't know why they taped Lena's eyes shut. Perhaps they didn't want her opening them to the horror that was her immediate past and her impending future. Perhaps, it was so the light didn't bother her.

"I don't know," I say.

I can now only see the top of Frances' head. She's beginning to slump and will go down quickly.

"Frances, go to bed."

Her head bobs. The bedroom where her husband sleeps is awfully far away.

"Go now before you pass out."

She stands.

I disconnect the call. It's the only way to be sure she'll go to bed.

Now what? I sit. I can't work. I sit at this table, and I stare at the clouds.

Do I like this table? Do I like any of our furniture? I can't believe I own all this stuff, unscratched, unsullied, unused until we sat, lay, or ate on it.

The first thing I bought was a salad dryer. My first and last confident purchase. How the hell do I know what my taste is? This table? It doesn't offend me, but of all the tables in the world, is this, "the one"? I like our bed; it's huge, even if it gives me a hernia trying to make it. This room, this whole fucking life, was created after C and I walked into endless stores and said this, that, that, and this. We went a little crazy. We probably could have done without a few that, that and that's — the guest bedroom for one. Kitted out, but so far, we've had no visitors. I tend to amble in there a couple of times a day. It's the only room without a balcony attached so I can stare directly down onto the street. This compulsion to look out the window onto nothing is a bit worrying. But the room, what with my disturbing the dust motes and atoms, at least knows it's not being ignored.

My life is now substantial. Nothing is propped up by a brick or held together with duct tape. I don't have to cover worn out armrests with equally frayed bits of cloth. Every pot in the kitchen is guaranteed to conduct heat evenly. My knives are surgeon sharp.

Nine days out of ten, I want to smash all this shit to bits or at the very least, leave a water stain and mar the sheen on this table, which is reflecting the underside of my chin—a sight no woman should ever have to see. But if you grow up in a ruin; you can't just start sitting primly and remember to use a coaster.

At least, it was an evolving ruin my childhood home. Although I never realised just how shabby it was until Granny Quick came to visit something she had avoided for years, waiting, I suppose to see if my parents were actually going to stay married.

Mother, having seen some Indian movie, had redone the whole house with an eye towards the Raj, replete with hanging couches and a riot of Indian bedspreads stapled up in the place of wallpaper. It was dizzying and disconcerting, and soon the sagging spreads provided all sorts of cover for various urban bugs. I remember Gran, breathless having climbed the stairs, seeing our home for the first time and me, ever the ambassador to my mother's madness, only too keen to demonstrate how the couches could swing not only back and forth but side to side sending one of them directly into her knee. Four times she had to go to the hospital to have the deep contusion drained.

I doubt anyone thought she'd cross the pond again.

But she did.

If only she had known.

Nobody is in a right frame of mind before her visit what with Daddy planning to leave, and the only thing mother can think to do is start the most appalling fights. They are never, though, about the one thing she dreads, losing him. On one night she threatens to throw herself down the stairs, and does let her body crumble down a stair or two. I can hear it all from my bedroom and am embarrassed for her. Everything she says leaves him cold. But she knows she went too far when at dinner she told Lena to fuck off. Now, she is desperate to make amends. Why? Why? She should be telling him to fuck off. Instead, she's clinging to his ankles. This after making dinner in a fucking heatwave so the family can plan to ensure there are no fuck-ups with Gran like last time.

"There's a lot of new things that might frighten Gran," Lena says, stabbing at her deracinated pork chop.

"Like what?" mother asks.

Both my parents' G&Ts are sweating, leaving wet patches on the tablecloth, the last of the Indian bedspreads, and the only one that hadn't ripped when torn from the walls.

Lena, mouth full, creates a suspended pause while she chews. Mother, not the most patient woman, shifts in her seat while pushing her hair off her face. I want more than anything for Lena to not chew her food down to a pulp even at the risk of choking because nothing annoys my father more than my mother's annoyance. Lena knows nothing of my parent's dissolving marriage, nothing of the nightly rows. She is always safely home.

"The bed…"

"Your father's idea…"

"The rug…"

"Again, your father…"

"And the hole in the wall…"

"Dad did that for you," I say.

That fucking hole. Cracked my head on it a million times, once even needed stitches, but Lena pointed out the back of the flat had no escape route should a fire break out, so Daddy promptly smashed a hole in the wall between the two rooms creating a portal.

Lena looks at me. "And I will tell Gran that. But I thought the hole would look better."

"Like the rug?" Mother asks.

My father frowns. The rug looked like shit. Once pure yellow, he had spilled a bottle of ink on it, and, rather than attempting to clean it, he went and got another bottle and, as he said, "splatter-dashed" the rest. It might have worked except the original spot was a dead zone of black ink, and the rest soon faded and bled, and the once yellow rug now just looked smudged, filthy, and grey.

Mother sighs, she looks, inexhaustibly sad. Downing the last of her drink, she gets up, goes over to the mirror above the non-working fireplace, and stares at herself for a long time before wondering (dully) when the hell Montreal got so damn humid. (Ha, Mother from the past! Try living in AD. You want humid!). Lena, watching her, waits a second before pointing out that it is humid because we live beside a river. Any large body of water is going to contribute to atmospheric conditions.

I, at least, am impressed with Lena's wealth of knowledge. Mother, not so much. She wheels around, her face contorted and says, "London is built on a river, a river along whose shores I spent my entire youth, a river that provided my father with a job as a dock worker, a river that regularly coughs up Roman coins, set men off on long sea voyages, harboured more than a few wayward whales and sucked my younger brother under on his eighth birthday no less, but never ever did it make an entire city feel like a fucking rotting biscuit! So fuck you, Lena, and your fucking theories."

Dad's G&T glass just misses her head, and before she realizes what has happened, he stands up and tells Lena he is taking her home.

After they are gone, mother rages, then seems contrite; when that doesn't sit well, she ends up stone-faced in the kitchen where she tells me that she might as well kill herself. Instead, when father gets back, she threatens to throw herself down the stairs. Bumpy beginnings for the still unknown Frances.

The heat has not abated the day Gran arrives, but there has been something of a truce between my parents. I put on my favourite dress, a cotton shift with straps that come over my bony shoulders and latched in front — my last little girl dress.

I watch from the window as my father bends his long frame into a British racing green Austin Healey to head for the airport, the car one of his clients who has asked him to test the gears. The gears are fine; even I can hear that. The client is just terrified of being blown up, shot at, or driven off the road by Quebec Separatists.

Sometimes, as the cavalcade of trucks carrying the weary workers back to their camp is rumbling past, I wonder if there will come a time of revolt. Seems unlikely, these poor buggers don't look like they have enough energy left to even dream about screwing a woman, let alone tipping the scale of power by striking or rioting. Montreal in the '60s and '70s wasn't so dishearteningly unbalanced, although pretty much every shit job was held by a skinny Québécois kept lithe by a steady diet of cigarettes and Pepsi. This is a cultural stereotype but for a little kid, a reassuring thing to hang onto. Us/them. I did harbour some jealousy: I wasn't allowed any soda of any kind. I didn't taste my first Coca-cola until I was nearly ten.

It didn't take the Anglos long to realize they are seriously outnumbered, and the fear is palpable. Mrs. Miller, across the street, will no longer allow the Québécois delivery boys from our local supermarket through her front door. Mother roars with laughter when they dump her boxes of groceries at the end of her walkway, where the hot sun makes quick work of her butter, ice cream, and packets of Spencer steaks.

Mother points out that taking a sport's car to pick up his mother is ridiculous but driving the Austin-Healey outweighs any impracticality. And, my father is in no mood to yield any ground to either his wife or his mother. His mistress is demanding enough. I know because she is in the habit of calling the house, and if I answer instead of Mother, who tends to slam the phone down, she pours out her frustrations. The last time she called, she confesses that she has bought an entirely new living room set so that my father won't have to sit on anything any other man has. "I am a beautiful woman. What did he think? That I was a virgin before we met?" Still, she went to Roche Bobois and bought a couch which, if she is honest, isn't that comfortable. And, what had he done? Allowed his mother to come for a visit.

I listen on the other end, offering no comment, but I am aware that both women in his life are not thrilled with Granny's visit. I am. While the last trip had been a bit of a disaster, I am her namesake, Augusta, which left me forever burdened with Augati, a diminutive that no one seems to know how to pronounce. Plus, I assume she will bring gifts.

As my father drives away, I realise that Lena won't be thinking of getting a present, she'll be making one. Something homemade, stunning in its handy work, considered, neither over the top nor strange. The only thing I ever gave my grandmother is my handprint in clay, but I missed the mark, so there are only four fingers and no thumb. The alien weirdness was lost on her.

Years ago, C and I lived for a while in Paris. One Sunday we went to the old Picasso Museum, now it's a huge thing, but then it was a sweet little museum stuffed with his shit. By the last room, I was beginning to think the guy had a problem. He left nothing alone. Broom handles, plates, toothbrushes, forks, chairs, everything was given the Picasso treatment. I could imagine Francoise or Jacqueline saying, "Pablo, For Christ's sake, leave it be, it's my sanitary napkin."

Lena is a bit like Picasso. She continually hems things, paints things, rearranges things. Plain white blouses are embroidered with delicate cross-stitching. One Christmas, she asks for a glass engraver, and soon all our drinking glasses are etched with flowers of every persuasion.

So, as I watch my father disappear I know at that moment in her other house, Lena is bent over some project that will please Gran no end.

Mother yells from the kitchen, her voice sharp and harried. I am starting to dread her voice and the tendrils of need that seem to add a physical weight that centres itself in the pit of my stomach. This feeling will become more pronounced as I grow older, so much so that there are times that being with her gave me a terrible stomach ache. Her extreme old age has one salutary effect; the stinger seems to have fallen off.

The kitchen is a mess. I stay in the doorway, not wanting my dress to come into contact with the flour, egg, and cheese mixture that somehow burst the banks and is now smeared across all the countertops. The fridge door gapes open, and the sink is clogged with various discarded aspects of whatever the hell my mother is attempting to cook.

A soufflé, it turns out.

She looks at me, her eyes wild. "I forgot the fucking cream of tartar." Her hands thick with flour and egg, she finds her purse, pulls out a ten-dollar bill and flings it at me. "Now, now, before it's too late." The barrage of threats when she sees me start to protest follows me out the door.

Only halfway down the street do I realize I am barefoot. The sidewalks are hot, the road hotter. But being a fleet-footed little fucker, I tear across the street, only to miss the curb. I stumble but do not fall.

C knows this story through and through. It's one of the ones trotted out through a long marriage, told mostly the same way. And it's always at this point that he stops the narration. It seems my running across that blazing hot road and nearly falling is indicative of my whole personality. "You bang your head, knees, and elbows more than seems possible. Set fire to endless tea towels. You walk through countless screen doors, not to mention, not one, but three glass doors. You have to stop moving through life like a lunatic." I nod. And then I pick up the thread of my story again.

But something has been lost in the myriad retellings. High jinks have countervailed the sense of foreboding. The first time I saw Antonioni's films and felt the spaces between the dialogue, the a priori knowledge of anxiety, of trying to communicate, all pitched up against the backdrop of Italy shaking itself out after the war years, I practically had a fit. That was what my eight-year-old brain couldn't see, or even conceive of on that day. Dissatisfaction swirled all around me. And what seemed ominous proved benign, and what seemed benign haunts me to this day.

As I stand, my feet stinging on the cold floors of the supermarket, I need Antonioni over my left shoulder. Need him to swing his camera around and let it rest on the perfect ass of the store manager, a beautiful woman who had recently had all her teeth removed, a prophylactic against future rot. I can only assume that that rage among Québécois to knock out their perfectly good teeth is yet another fuck you to us Anglos, with our Queen, our high teas, and our fabled bad teeth.

She turns. Her sunken face revived by an even set of dentures.

"Cream of tartar?"

"Comment?" The woman clicks her tongue, turns away, and starts hitting all the cigarette boxes, so they line up perfectly. I wait. She turns back. "Crème de tartare?" she spits. Ducking now from behind the counter, she takes off at a quick clip, her heels clicking, giving a stock boy's bottom a tap as she passes, smiling her pale-denture smile. In front of the spices, she scans the display, touching a pencil she'd taken from behind her ear along each of the little spice bottles as she mutters under her breath with machine-gun rapidity: crème de tartare, crème de tartare. When her pencil hits on it, she flips it out and tosses it to me while giving me a once over that now stops abruptly at my feet.

"Tu saignes!"

I follow the woman's accusing pencil. My big toe. It is bleeding profusely, and the nail is more than half off.

"What the fuck!"

I look up. Heather.

Unable to move, the floor around me is quickly starting to become sticky with blood spreading out like those bad graphics of Soviet terror spreading its red Commie menace across Europe. The manageress takes a step back, her hand reachs out and Heather, a slight smile on her face, takes hold of it. "Vous ne pouvez pas saigner!" she says, now pulling Heather in close. "Vas t' en. Merde!"

"She's telling you to get the fuck out of here," Heather says.

Mother. Down on her knees, furious, the bleeding not stopping, the bathroom steamy hot, and the part in her hair glistening with sweat. At least, I fled with the cream of tartare. I hold it still.

"Why in god's name were you running?"

"The road was hot and…"

"And what?"

"And nothing."

"Stand up!"

"Why?"

"I have to see something."

"If you're thinking the nail will fall off, it won't." I lean forward, "See that one bit there; it's still attached."

"Oh, for fuck's sake. I've never seen such a ridiculous thing." Mother sits back on her haunches. "And Heather saw you like this?"

"It's not my fault."

"Of course, it is."

"Just leave it. I'll put the band-aid on."

"Well, you might have said."

Mother stands, her knees cracking, and gives a quick glance in the mirror. There is the rebuke. Of herself, of me, the clumsy daughter who has shown her up once again. She takes the tin of cream of tartare out of my hand and leaves the bathroom.

Alone, I bend over, breathing in the gamey smell of my summer-scuffed knees and assess the damage. The nail needs to be pulled off, but there is no fucking way I'd find the courage to do that. All I can manage is to lay it back into place. The first band-aid I gingerly wrap around my toe didn't seem nearly enough, and the pain I hadn't felt in the store is starting to be all-consuming. My toe throbs with a manic life force. I put on another band-aid and another till the box is nearly empty, and my toe is encased like Chernobyl.

I stay sitting on the edge of the bathtub, the bloodied kleenexes, and towels needing to be picked up. I stay staring at my toe, my chin resting on my knees — all that pain, all that throbbing, invisible. I want something more. Something like Heather has. To be there, in control, a watcher. Instead, I am a young idiot in the blender, whipping around, spraying blood. I dread standing up, walking out, and seeing mother. We both know. Then I remember that Lena is going to be collected after Gran had been picked up at the airport. The three would arrive together. Lena would have given Gran her welcome present.

I hobble out of the bathroom in time to see mother throw her soufflé in the garbage.

"It smelled like shit. Like rotten fucking eggs."

"I'm not going back to the store."

"Have I asked you to?"

I sit down at the table.

"There must be something in the freezer."

Mother goes over to the fridge. She tosses aside some ancient frozen roasts and pellet-hard packages of chicken bones saved for soups never made.

"Nothing."

She grabs the vodka bottle before slamming the door closed and goes out onto the balcony, slumping down in the old wicker chair, its seat mostly gone. I join her and stare down onto Chesterfield Ave, forlorn, and deserted. Most of the families have decamped to the country, leaving their small front lawns to run to brown. There has been humidity, but there hasn't been any rain in weeks. All is still, except mother.

"Well," she says, struggling out of the chair, "we'd bloody well better come up with something to eat before your sister arrives with an Audubon tracing or a hand-knit coaster. There's a tube of liverwurst; it will have to do."

Eventually, I find it too hot on the balcony and hop back into the kitchen to find her listlessly dabbing at a mound of pâté.

"This looks disgusting."

"What's it supposed to be?"

"A light repast."

I suggest she puts some pickles around it. There are only two left in the jar. Mother sticks her whole hand in and fishes them out, thinly slicing them on an angle and then arranges the pieces across the liverwurst.

"What went wrong with the soufflé?"

"You took too long with the cream of tartar. It fell."

"Fell where?"

"Unto itself," she says, pushing her hair off her face with her forearm, pickle juice running into her eyes. "Fuck! For Christ's sake, Aug, do something useful."

"Like what?"

Squinting, mother looks around.

"Open those tins of soup."

"Soup? It's a million degrees."

"Just do as you're told."

Leaning halfway across the table, no longer caring what state my dress is in, I pull the tins of minestrone towards me and start to open them.

"This is more like lunch than dinner."

"It will be midnight in London when we eat."

I felt a stab then. What little I knew about the world didn't include the vagaries of time. Lena would explain later how time zones worked and that if a person wanted, they could leave a place and fly over a whole day so that when they landed, they were two days older. That, and why we never see the dark side of the moon, took me forever to figure out. From grade seven onward, I failed math consistently, as if that explains anything.

"Your grandmother won't want a big meal so late."

"But I'll be hungry. It won't be midnight here."

"There'll be toast points."

I push one tin of soup aside and begin opening another. Toast points doesn't sound promising.

"How many of these should I open?"

"All of them."

"Five cans?"

"There are five of us."

"Lena doesn't eat a whole tin. She never does."

"Screw, Lena. This is a bistro dinner. What does she know of French bistro cooking?"

"Nothing, I guess."

"Exactly."

I start on another can. "I thought minestrone was Italian."

"Your grandmother," she says, "is a suburban English woman of a certain age who wouldn't know minestrone from Vichyssoise. So stop asking so many bloody questions."

She begins to jam bread in the toaster for her toast points. I know now she was scared. Hours away from another visit from Augusta Quick, never an ally. Though to be fair, Granny knew what sort of son she had. She did years later write a conciliatory letter to Mother when my father married his fourth wife. "I thought Liv made a perfectly good wife, but since that wasn't to be, you were fine." I found that letter when I was packing up mother's things. It had been balled up in a rage, then smoothed out again.

Her mound of liver pâté draped in flaccid pickles would have to wait until Liv got to see her ex-mother-in-law first. Liv, the adorable war orphan, who, by fate, ended up being billeted with the Quicks. A little miracle who had already survived the bombing of Rotterdam, had traveled, a girl alone, to the far shores of England but never asked for pity, never cried for her mother (both parents squashed by a falling wall) never made any sort of fuss. She liked to help in the kitchen, liked to watch the rambunctious Quick boys roughhouse, and even found a way to steal Miles Quick's heart. Of course, Augusta loved Liv and Lena. Way more than us.

"Are you going to be in a bad mood the whole time Gran is here?"

Mother raises the plate high before smashing it to the floor. The liverwurst stays solid.

"There. Look what you've done."

I charge her in a blind fury while she was still staring down at the broken plate and mound of pâté. A mad scamp, clawing, biting, kicking, which sent alarm bells of pain tearing up my leg. She bats me away the best she can, but her vodka-addled arms render nothing but pathetic blows. Before I am spent, we hear from down below the low rumble of the Healey.

Next thing, I am sobbing into the folds of my grandmother's dress, aware, acutely, that her breasts are huge and her stomach soft. Lena stands watching. I am surprised she hasn't offer an explanation for my behaviour; she usually had one on hand. Granny probably wants to crawl back into that ridiculous little car and beg my father to take her back to the airport.

Not knowing what had transpired when they went to pick up Lena, I tend to think of Gran's arrival as if I am looking down on it from on high. Lena, small, neat, her hair in braids with her welcome poster rolled up, held so loosely that it threatened to fall; she is alone. My tears, our grandmother's increasing impatience with this snotty child clinging to her, my father slamming about, pulling oversized suitcases from the trunk of the Healey, Lena watches it all as if she is behind glass or an alien who feels nothing for a bewildering host of what seem like nonsensical emotions. This, I fear, was the moment when Lena was lost to me, where, everything shifted, and she was being pulled inexorably towards the full knowledge that we, her family, couldn't save her.

This tableau is broken up by mother coming downstairs and prying me off my poor grandmother.

There will be no tour. Lena and I follow Mother as she hustles Augusta upstairs and straight through to the kitchen, where she immediately pours Gran a drink she obviously doesn't want. I suppose if any of us had a mind to other people's wants and needs, we would have seen that what Gran wants is for the strange events that she has witnessed since landing to disappear. And, she needs a cup of tea and a bath, preferably one in a bathroom that isn't strewn with wads of blood-soaked tissues and towels.

"Kick that back, and we'll get dinner downtown," Mother says, handing Gran a formidable vodka and tonic, and then joining her at the table. "Did you get a chance to see Liv?"

Lena and I are standing in the doorway of the kitchen, she grabs my hand; her grip as vivid now as it was painful then.

I give an involuntary cry. Granny snaps around. "No more hysterics, please."

Gran, not a big woman, but always upright, sits slumped in the chair, her arm resting on the table. Even Mother stops to take note. We are all silent a moment before Mother says we should go and help Miles bring up Gran's bags.

At the top of the outside stairs, I am about to take hold of the banister so I can hop down, but Lena shows no sign of wanting to move. She stands there, weaving slightly. I wonder now if she was thinking of falling forward, her compact frame no match for the steep stairs.

She isn't looking at me. She doesn't seem to be looking at anything. "Mum and I were at the window," she says, "when Dad and Gran arrive to pick me up. Before Dad had a chance to honk, Heather, wearing one of my mum's skirts and a jacket, heels and I think her pearls too, was suddenly there. Right by the car. She waited a moment before rapping on the window. When Dad rolled it down, she raised her skirt. She wasn't wearing underwear. I could see her bum as she shoved...right into Daddy's face."

I turn to her. All is silent until Lena whispers, "Her thing, in his face."

"What did you do?"

"Nothing."

"What did your mother do?"

"Nothing. Heather ran off down the street."

"But she's going to get into trouble, right?"

Lena looks at me blankly before starting down the stairs. I hop after her.

What could the punishment have been? Liv was not the sort of woman to haul any of her children in by the scruff of the neck and give them a good thrashing. You might scold a toddler or a young child for their forensic interest in a playground game of "I'll show you mine if you show me yours." But Heather was twelve, nearly thirteen the most I could imagine Liv doing is taking her Chanel suit to the cleaners and perhaps locking her rope of pearls in the safe she and Piers had in their bedroom.

I was once at a rowdy party in one of those quintessential Montreal triplexes that have balconies in front. A boy vaulted over the railing and at first hung like a monkey; then, he let go, so his fingers were grasping the edge. What happened to him? I was there and yet have no memory of him finding enough of a hold to get back up. He couldn't have fallen; he would have died. Something so vivid, so burned on my brain, has no next moment. Over the years, I have imagined that's how Liv must have reacted. Her daughter sticks her cunt in her ex-husband's face, out on the street for all to see. From there, there is no next moment, not one that makes any sense.

My father's temper is indication enough of how unnerved he is. One of Gran's bags, the one, it turns out, which contains two porcelain dolls, he kicks along the pavement until he reaches the stairs, then he picks it up and hurls it only to have it come bumping back down. Lena watches, silent and grave. She will never mention what has happened ever again, at least not to me. And more weirdly, I don't go running up the stairs crying, "Mum! Mum! Heather stuck her thing in Dad's face!"

We are a strange, secret-holding group that finally gathers on the back balcony to have a few drinks before heading downtown for dinner. Lena sits, the one potato chip taken when offered, growing limp in her hand. My father keeps losing the thread of the conversation, not that there is much of one.

Her thing. That thing. My thing. All these things, even before I saw Heather at the supermarket, even before Lena told me what had happened, were the only things I thought about. Obliquely. Obsessively. But in the realm, realm of romance, of small kisses, of hand holding. Things I wanted. Though, I know my "thing" was leading these desires. Shattered. All those things, that moment, out on the balcony has been ruined, made dirty, shameful. I am scared. I could tell everyone else is scared. Except, mother, she is merely drunk. But then she doesn't know.

Doesn't know anything.

When she reaches for yet another drink, Gran, her voice weary and furious, asks. "Should you be drinking so much?"

My father tips his chair back. He isn't going to defend his wife.

"I'm not wrong, Mab, am I?" Gran says, pressing. "You are going to have a baby?"

"What?" My father looks first to Gran, sees she is serious, and then to Mother. "How the hell did that happen?"

Mother flushes deeply, and then instantly knows. "Oh, my god!"

"You couldn't tell?"

"I thought I was menopausal."

"This beggars belief."

"The children…"

"For God's sake, Mother, shut up. Bloody hell, Mab, how could any woman be so completely unaware of her own body?"

"I wasn't unaware; I just got it wrong."

"How far along do you think the bloody thing is?"

Five months, it turns out.

C just called there's some screw up with our visas. We have to go back down to immigration and get fingerprinted again. The problem is, I have no fingerprints to give. They have either been worn away by age or burned off from picking up hot pots and pans. Last time I had to go to a special department where there was a machine sensitive enough to pick up my faded whorls and swirls.

I am ridiculously put out. I yelled at C on the phone, as if it was his fault. Broke down in tears. He got impatient and hung up on me. It is only immigration, a morning, but it's also here, right here, my family, drinks in hand, caught between the two equally shocking antipodes of Heather's thing in my father's face and a baby, who would be Frances, who, two seconds before, none of us had any clue about.

So it is with some relief that we leave the balcony, not that we are a cohesive whole heading out into the hazy summer evening what with me trailing behind having to hop slowly down the stairs and Mother having to rush back up because she forgot her purse. My father pulls the Land Rover around. I don't know if he and his mother exchange a look but they both must be thinking the same thing: high tires, high chassis, high windows and high door. Had he picked her up from the airport in the Rover, the quick lift of Heather's skirt would have missed its mark or been unseen altogether.

The truck is musty and very hot. My father opens the air vents and then declares that the tires seem squishy. I think of my barefoot charge across the road. The tar so soft, I felt like I was sinking. We are silent as he fills the tank and puts air in the tires. Silent too as he circles the slate grey warrens of Old Montreal looking for a parking spot.

The Creperie, a place with bulbous stone walls, low ceilings and waitress' wearing towering lace head dresses and puffy skirts, is a winter place with its intoxicating smell of warm butter and maple syrup. Even so, it is full, and on the way to our table, we pass a large birthday party. I spy a girl my age wearing white go-go boots and a leather mini skirt. God, I want those boots. She is the only one who doesn't have a helium balloon attached to her wrist, which, as the party grows more boisterous, are pulled down and sucked on to great and giddy hilarity.

Mother, unsteady on her feet, knocks over a glass of water as we all are pulling out chairs and trying to decide who should sit where. Lena, Gran and I grab for napkins to sop up the mess as my father hisses, "Leave it. Leave it. Let the bloody waitress do her job."

Drinks are ordered and we bend over our menus with concentration. When mother's gin and tonic arrives, she throws away her swizzle stick and lime and says, "I have no doubt that the mood was rather more celebratory when your mother found out she was pregnant with you, Lena. Not that you'd remember, of course. And, what did your father know of babies then?"

Lena stares fixedly at the table. Only a fortnight before she had been told to "Fuck off."

My father reaches out and tousles her head. She sinks lower in her chair.

A balloon pops. Granny jumps and grabs her chest.

Our crêpes arrive.

Mother pushes her plate away. "I remember when Liv and Piers went up to Newfoundland to pick up Heather and Leslie. It was just before Christmas. Why wait, these babies must have a real Christmas! The pride your mother took in her cards that year. Leslie did look a bit peculiar, slumped, drooling, her eyes closed. But what should you expect? You were lovely though, Lena and, of course, Heather, bloody stunning. That too was a celebration."

Gran excuses herself. Her crepe, ham and cheese, untouched, and goes to the ladies room.

Father growls. "Mab, for Christ's sake."

But another round of helium hilarity allows her to pretend she hasn't heard him. She takes a swig of her drink rattling her ice. Lena grips the sides of the table to quell a tremor created by my jiggling leg. But I am not told to stay still. Or cuffed.

Mother leans forward, elbow on table, her chin nestled in her hand, her gaze unfocused, "With you, Augati. Well, you. I knew the second I conceived." she pauses, then says slowly, "Con-cep-tion."

I look at Lena; her knuckles white against the rough wooden table, stewed apples and fast melting vanilla ice cream seeping out of her crepe. I stop my leg, but it starts up again. I am edged by a half-formed impulse but have no idea what I wish I could do. Stop my jittering leg? Eat Lena's crepe? Steal the white go-go boots off that other girl's feet? Un-drunk mother? Understand? Yes, if only I can understand but I am eight, the incomprehensible stays just that, there is no reference, no history, no words to help me.

"And what about this little blighter? Miles? What?"

Mab puts her hand on her stomach, her first acknowledgment of the life within.

My father starts to cry. It takes a moment for the three of us to realise what is happening. Mother bites her lip, bangs her head with a clenched fist before reaching out a forgiving hand. But her gesture is ignored. He stays, his head down, the sobs slowing to a punctuated shudder.

When Gran returns, she takes one look at her son and sits down heavily. For a woman who has come through two world wars, raised her children, lost her husband, the trials and griefs are narrow and to be gotten through. But since getting off the plane a mere four hours ago, she has been roughly tipped into confusion, and fear. What is this madness that had seized her son's family, even though Heather wasn't family, Liv was, would always be, no matter how many wives Miles drags in. And, with the news of the baby, with her son, now, blowing his nose, gathering himself, she isn't entirely sure anymore of what she had witnessed. It was only a second, after all. A knock on the window. She turns and there, there. Chances are it didn't happen but then, she knows, it isn't something that she could ever have imagined.

And what of Lena? Sliding down to the edge of my own chair, reaching as far as I can with my good foot, I try to nudge her but she must have her feet tucked under. There will be no secret concord. She is no longer gripping the table but now has her hands laid gently in her lap. A blank. A void. How wrong I was. Her animal instinct? Camouflage. She was not to be seen. Clearing our plates, the busboy, forgets hers.

We get up to leave but are held up by the arrival of a blazing birthday cake and the singing of Happy Birthday. Mother grabs our waitress by the arm and says, "Sounds like a fucking funeral dirge, don't you think?"

The waitress yanks her arm away.

Once home, we all retreat to our own rooms. Later, as I head to the bathroom I can hear the clipped tones of my parents behind their bedroom door.

Brushing my teeth, I want to think about the baby and what it might mean--I have no idea except the vaguely formed worry that I, of all the girls, will soon have a whole sister—but find instead my mind obsessively wandering over to the image of Heather thrusting her cunt into my father's face. Ducking to drink from the tap, I realize that Heather's actions were not directed at him at all, but at Lena. But why? Yet again, I have no path towards understanding.

Lena is in bed when I get back from the bathroom, lying neatly under the one cotton sheet. She is watching me.

"Are you going to leave your toe like that?"

"Yeah, why?"

"Because you'll get gangrene."

"What's that?"

"It's when a wound is not allowed to breathe, goes black, smells like rotten eggs, and your toe falls off. You'd better sleep with your foot outside the cover just in case. You should have ripped off the nail. Then it would be healing already."

Healing? The damn thing is still sending shock waves up my leg. I can't tell you the panic I feel at the prospect of my toe falling off, which now considering the pain, is all but certain. Lena rolls over and goes to sleep, leaving me sitting on the edge of the bed, contemplating a toeless future.

Finally, I get up again and limp back into the bathroom. If nothing else I have to see what is happening beneath my mound of bandages.

The first five come off relatively easily, but with the last one, I feel a sickening tug.

"What's happening here?"

I look up. There, framed in the doorway, is my father.

"Lena said I'd get gangrene."

"Did she?"

He kneels down. I shrink back.

"Don't be a bloody idiot. I'm not going to touch it. I just want to check your bandage."

Gingerly, I offer him my foot which, he takes and cradles as if he were about to slip a shoe on.

"Not bad," he nods. "Perhaps though we should put on one more?"

"Really?"

"I should think so. Look up there," he says, jerking his head towards the shelf over the sink, "and see if there are any more band-aids."

The next moment, the two of us are staring down at my nail-less toe, shining red over pearly white. My father's grip still vice-like around my foot.

"There," he says "Wasn't that easy?"

IRA. Baader-Meinhof. FSLN, the FARC. And, what about that muddle of gangs ringing Burma, or rather Myanmar? Who else? The Weathermen? And, they actually managed to blow themselves up. Then there's ISIS and Al Qaeda, and probably as I sit here, some new faction is being sprung into life, new blood to an old story, and they too are seeking to blow themselves up, along with the rest of us.

I'll think of more. Nothing else to do while I wait. The suspect? A trailing spouse with no discernible fingerprints. What might I be planning? There is no way to give one's prints without feeling the weight of criminal history. Our fingers, the breadcrumbs that led countless cops to our doorsteps. Though with Heather, she left a trail of blood. Trail. Trailing. I am innocent. She was not. Yet I am here, watched by cameras, waiting to be scanned. There was a moment, with C in the male only side of the building getting his prints lifted, that I thought I might have just enough evidence of myself but in the end, it was hopeless, my print taker and I staring dumbly at the screen as she rolled my flat-line pads back and forth trying to capture an image.

C let out a long sigh when I emerged and shook my head. I am a constant source of worry. I break out in body-covering hives at odd moments. I once had an itchy brain. One leg is significantly longer than the other, so I tend to walk into things and suffer the bruises. Like most men, this angers him first before he reaches out, with a half frown, wanting to know why. Why I'm not more careful? Why does my body seem to have a mind of its own? But having no fingerprints is by far the most upsetting. It says something about me that he can't quite put his finger on. Am I an alien? Do I not exist?

C and I walked over here together, not speaking, the heat too intense, but he was forbidden to enter, so now waits for me in a faux French cafe in Al Wahda Mall. I, in the meantime, am sitting on a hardback chair idly biting my nails tallying up terrorists and rebel groups, bombs and bombers.

I thought I was going to get blown up, which might be worse than actually being blown up. These days there doesn't seem to be the warnings. Now with bombs squirrelled beneath jackets or hidden in backpacks, only the bomber knows what's about to happen, and, I gather, he's all for it. But to know, to think, to wait? It's a panic beyond what our minor senses can cope with. It stills you. Extends time. Although, if you believe you are heading towards Allah or are cloaked in some other messianic belief, does that speed things up? Who the fuck knows.

My bomb. Our bomb. A bomb that turned out, in the end, not to exist. But what did Lena and I know? We got the call: you're going to get blown up. You tend to believe the most improbable.

I have watched Get Smart, Green Acres and, The Beverly Hillbillies. American shows that don't quite make sense to me knowing nothing about Texas Oil or the 5th Avenue fashions that Eva Gabor had to abandon, or the cold war, for that matter. Now bored, I head to the kitchen, stepping over the dried trampled troughs that were used to wet the wallpaper my father had been putting up in the baby's room, an exercise that so infuriated him he had left the job half done, and gone on a three-day bender. As I come into the kitchen Lena, her hair neatly tucked behind her ears, points at the phone and tell me to answer it.

Before I even said, "Hello," a man's voice bears down on me.

Sitting here on this hardback chair, surrounded by the muffled murmuring of women beneath the veil, waiting to be fingerprinted, deemed a non-hostile, that voice booms in my head. Lena knew, saw it all in my face as she takes the phone from me. She understands what he is saying and drops the receiver only to retrieve it and slam it into the cradle, the phone's bell reverberating.

"What?"

"There is a bomb in the house."

We shrink back as the flat hunches up and grows large with the impending threat.

I am frozen with panic and had Lena not yelled at me; I still might be standing there, caught forever wild-eyed. Your shoes! Get your shoes. I look down at my stocking feet. (Why am I never wearing shoes when big terrible things happen in my life?) My shoes? They could be anywhere, always kicked off unthinkingly. I run into the living room, which smells faintly of toast and scotch, no shoes. I run into my room where nearly lost under my bed are my school lace-ups. Not bothering to untie them, I slip my left foot in, but my right one won't go.

"Augati!" Lena screams from the front door.

"My shoe! It won't go!" I can see what I am doing wrong, jamming my foot straight down, but I can't help myself. In frustration, I bite my hand. Finally, I just crush down the back. That shoe, nearly slipped off and sent me flying down the stairs as we make our escape.

Out on the street, we stop and out of bomb range, aware, on that cold November evening, of all the houses around us, secure, idle, indifferent and, warm.

I ask how long it take for a bomb to go off. Lena thinks a moment and then says it all came down to whether there was a clock attached, a timer.

"Did the man say?"

"No."

We look up the street and then down, but it is starkly devoid of anyone who might help. I need to pee badly. Lena is not coming up with a plan, the opposite; she is lost.

"The police? Should we call the cops?" I said. Although, the police arriving more than a few times during the worst of my parent's fights were usually not a welcome presence.

"How?" Lena asked.

"We could go to your house."

"No."

"Why?"

"Just no."

"But why?"

"We just can't. Piers wouldn't like it."

"What?"

"Under no circumstances are you allowed in our house."

"But..."

That "but" should have been given full range and outrage. No circumstances? Not even being blown up? But there was no time and the wound of that revelation wouldn't fester until years later.

"Mum's phone stretches."

I look at her. She is serious. I take off up the stairs where I push the inside door so hard that it springs back in my face. Mother's phone cord does stretch and I get the phone halfway down the hallway where Lena is waiting. She dials O and then speaks calmly and deliberately as she tells the operator what has happened. Before she has even rung off, police sirens can be heard. We clatter back downstairs. I wish then for something, not death-inducing, but enough to warrant all the fuss.

Two sets of cops arrive. Our local Westmount police and the much more menacing Montreal police. They have a shotgun resting in the front seat of their patrol car. And no interest in speaking to two little girls, which leaves the Westmount police to question us.

The flashing lights has brought most of the neighbours to their windows. Nobody, though, comes out to see what was up or if we are in any trouble.

"Was he French?" one cop presses.

Of course, he spoke fucking French. But Lena isn't going to tell him that. I know what the housewives, standing sentinel by their windows, think of us. But I know too what they think of the Québécois disrupting the natural order of things, their stifling closed world, thick with gin and boredom, which they will hold onto to their dying breaths. Yeah, it was a fucking Quebecker targeting us to target them.

"French, yes, he spoke French," I burst out. "They want to blow up my mother. They said it. In the paper, the French paper. They said that."

I can feel Lena behind me, willing me to be silent.

"Why did they say that?" The cop asks.

All sorts of things jam into my head—the Queen's charred picture in the post office. FLQ and English Dogs Out scrawled across bus shelters. And mother! Well, father screaming at mother that, "The bloody Separatists didn't give a shit that she thought their cause was about the only interesting thing happening in Canada, in Montreal, they saw her as the enemy. She wasn't going to pretend she wasn't British, was she? That would be a fucking lark. She was about as British as they came?" To which, she replied, "I'm mostly Irish," To which he roared, "They don't give a shit, you are the imperial mascot if they ever saw one!" Mother usually ended this conversation with a "Fuck you."

It was too much.

"Because she's bloody British!" I shout. The sobs come unbidden as does pissing my pants. Lena stays stone-like behind me.

"There is no bomb." One of the Montreal cops materializes before us. "We checked all the places and found nothing. Remember, it is not so easy to make a bomb go boom."

He nods to the Westmount cops, who now close their books, get in their car and speed away.

The phone is still on the floor. Two men have been there, and they have touched everything. The flat has shifted, been invaded, rummaged through, and then carefully replaced, but everything is off by a degree or two. And, then there is that smell: intense, cologned, smoky. I think of mother's underwear drawer. Girdles, tangled pantyhose, old panties that she calls her "period knicks," shabby bras and a diaphragm, always snapped shut, on top of which lay a half-used tube of spermicide

A man's hand, stained yellow from cigarettes, has roamed over all of these things looking for something suspicious and in doing so has made everything in that drawer, everything, in fact, in the whole house, different.

"Do you feel safe?" Lena asks.

Is she kidding? The chair, the humidifier wheezing in the hallway, the TV still on in the living room, are all witness and victim.

"We will go to every room," Lena says, stepping over the threshold, "and stand holding our breath for twenty seconds just listening to see if we hear any ticking. After that, we'll look under every mattress and pillow because those things could muffle the sound."

"I can't."

Lena levels her eyes at my pissed soaked jeans. "Doesn't that burn?"

I learned then, I know now, that when facing possible annihilation, or at the very least, the dawning reality of parallel truths, there is always something else that snags the mind, the eye. My thighs were aflame with cold piss; it was unbearable.

We stop at the door to my room, four ears pricked noting as the radiator begins to knock and ping, hear the incessant rattle of the sash window as the evening winds pick up, and note the sweep of the Place Ville Marie searchlight sounding an audible swish as it arcs across the ceiling.

"Ticking?"

Lena shake her head.

Stepping gingerly into the room, I peel off my jeans and underwear. Then, expecting my hand to alight on the cold intent of a bomb, I pull out my pajamas from beneath my pillow and slip on the bottoms.

Room by room we go, faithfully holding our breath until we are back in the kitchen, Lena's homework still on the table. The flat, thoroughly purged, seems to simmer down, or merely assume a normal shape.

My palms still jump to sweat when I think of Lena and I standing in front of the open fridge-- hunger too pops up even in the midst of terror— when the phone sprang into life. We clung to each other, whimpering with fear, convinced our next breath would be our last. I can't remember who reached for it first, but we are side by side listening together when we heard our father shouting down the line, "What took you so bloody long? The baby's born. It's a bloody girl!"

Then the phone went dead. Still bent towards the receiver, we stood listening to the dial tone. Frances was here. There are press clippings that mother saved, not about the birth, but the bomb scare. The English papers were full of recriminations claiming that Quebec had reached the end of civil discourse. Fat chance. The battle for separation was just heating up; it would be years before it was at a full boil, years that corresponded with our family's own disintegration.

I seem to be the last one waiting.

I wonder if this room feels it's in its normal shape, an official office, one determined to do what all the other rooms and buildings in this newly built city do; try and make sense out of the senselessness of springing up in a barren desert. Are the cleaning crews at night spooked? No ghosts. Just the omnipresent triad of portraits of the

UAE founder and present rulers. One, his eyes, not as bad as Leslie's, but still strangely focused. You are watched here.

I can feel the heat of this woman's hand. And kindness. I apologize for being the last one waiting. And explain that it is my fault that I have no fingerprints. But she assures me that her screening machine will pick up what the other machines missed. I like her. We are joking around. I tell her that perhaps I should turn to a life of crime.

"Praise Allah, you don't do such a thing."

"Me? Do I look like the sort?"

She gives me the once over while gently rolling my fingertips back and forth across the screen. They find you by the eyes, she now tells me. Of course, they do. The machine beeps, all ten digits have been captured as well as a photo of my eyes. "Blue," she says, leaning over to shut off the machine.

I hear the security guard lock the door behind me. I need to get to C. It's way past cocktail hour. I am encased in heat and surprised anyone can walk upright under this weight of air-bound water. Outside the mall, there is a queue of people with their weekly shopping waiting for taxis. An old man wearing a vest, Trolley Boy, unloads their groaning carts into the taxi's trunk in a matter of seconds. Some tip. Some don't.

The blast of air conditioning hitting me as I enter the mall would be a godsend if there wasn't also that overwhelming smell of oud. There is always that tiny panic, what if C has disappeared? No need to wonder why that is. But he's here, I can see him. Head down, playing with his ear, reading. He hasn't seen me yet. So I get that moment, a lover's treat, to observe anew what will never be too familiar, too known. Thirty years and C is still heart-stoppingly beautiful.

The day my mother brought Frances home, while we all stared down at this swaddled child, there was a loud thump of something landing on the balcony. My father who said it was most likely a bird bashing into the window went to investigate. Mother lay a hand on Frances' forehead; there's one thing she fears, birds and their portent of death. It was a joke the bomb he held, a Westclox Silver Bell alarm clock with two fat fire crackers attached as sticks of dynamite, thrown up on to our balcony, but its effect was explosive enough.

Swearing, my father threw it in the garbage and then went and stood sentinel at the window, hoping to catch out the fake bomb thrower. But the street was barren. We ate dinner later that night with the faintly ticking clock in the garbage and, to me, at least, the unfamiliar sound of the caught and carried breaths of a newborn baby.

C has seen me. He points to his non-existent watch and then skyward. Yes, I nod, time to head to the hotel's rooftop bar.

"**H**ello? Hello? Frances, can you hear me? Fuck. Call me back if you can hear me. I can't hear you."

"Frances? Hello? There you are."

"Sit still; you're all pixelated."

"So are you."

"Call me back this time."

"Hello?"

I shouldn't be getting impatient. There are nearly ten thousand miles between us. It is her morning — my night. My image is going up into space, arcing around the curve of the earth and coming back down in L.A. to find Frances.

"Hello?"

"Finally."

Frances and, beside her on the couch, Mother, who keeps squinting at her own image.

"I tried you before, where were you?"

"Out having a drink with this guy who said he wanted to write about Marcelo."

"Why the fuck would anyone want to write about Marcelo?"

"He's a taste-maker."

Mother rolls her eyes.

"Turns out it wasn't Marcelo he was interested in. His wife is Beth Matthews."

"Who?"

"Beth? From my French class? The one who always sat beside Leslie? I know that look so fucking well, that hesitation. The "I was wondering..." Of course, he was wondering. Anybody who was in Montreal, even Canada, in the '70s when they meet me wonders, is she? Was she? To fuck with him, I pretended I didn't know her."

"Great. But who is she?"

"Beth. Mum, do you remember her?

"Can't say I do."

"I knew her in high school when Heather, Lena, Leslie and I are finally in the same school, at the same time. Beth and Leslie are in my French class, sit opposite me. Leslie all stooped, freckled, gawky, cross-eyed, desperate in every way. I can't see Beth's face, a non-face, face.

They are as bad at French as I am. Our teacher, Madame Forté, is this elegant, long-necked, Québécois woman. Her neck is so thin that when she grows impatient, which is every five seconds, her jugular vein pops out."

"Did you say, Forté?"

"Yes, why?"

"They thought she was a spy. At least, some of the Westmount mothers did. Rumours swirled about her. How ridiculous. What on earth could she find out from seventh graders? But later it was revealed that she had been part of the FLQ, and had suffered the humiliations of a lousy love affair with some top brass. She sought refuge in the quiet confines of Westmount High. Seems insane. Who would seek solace among teenagers?"

"I never heard that."

"That would be more likely than a spy."

"In any case, she has to deal with us idiots. Simple phrases, we thoroughly mangle. She survives until one day Beth, no matter how slowly she is asked, "C'est quand votre anniversaire?" can not say her birthday. The room is held spellbound as she sits stupidly blinking, which made Forté's sudden eruption all the more startling.

"Merde!" she screams. Then she stands, knocking her chair back and, unable to take another second in the presence of us morons, storms from the room, slamming the door behind her."

"Good for her."

"Mother, you like anyone who behaves as you would."

She ignores Frances' dig. "Imagine if I had put you in that full immersion school?"

"I would probably know how to speak French." I say.

Mother shrugs.

"So what happened to Beth?"

"She starts to whimper. Leslie reaches out and puts a hand on her shoulder. It is the only sound and movement in the room but beneath a volcanic energy runs through all of us. Any second I think I might leap up and start haring around the room like a crazy person, banging my head into the walls. The kid next to me must feel the same way. His leg involuntarily jolts out, sending his untied sneaker across the circle. But it was Billy, Billy Underhill."

"Billy. Shit." Frances says, her eyes widening.

"I know. He was the single focus of my hot-loined compass."

"You like those scrawny rangy guys."

"Yeah, and he came from a fucked-up Irish family. All of them mouthy. It is Billy who speaks first.

'What the fuck? Was that a frog thing?' he says.

I want more than anything for Billy to come over and pinch me, or slap me, something.

'A frog on the rag,' another kid says.

Billy stands, purposely knocking back his chair, and in an exaggerated tiptoe, goes up to the classroom door and peeks through the window. The hallway is empty and beckoning. We, this once quivering lumpish mass struck dumb by beginners' French, could leave and beat the rest of the school to freedom by a good fifteen minutes. Billy opens the door and holds up his hand.

'Run to the main doors and, if an alarm sounds, head across the playing field and down the hill,' he says. You would think we were escaping Alcatraz. We are so hopped up.

Then from the back.

'Maybe we shouldn't.'

Leslie. Speaking up for probably the first time in her life.

'Yeah, maybe we shouldn't,' Beth pipes in.

I have never felt such instant hatred. The fucking Driscoll family with their rules. The Friday night steak and chips. The homework hours. The daily baths to clean their undercarriage. Liv with her brushed coat and Lena with her labeled clothes, all of that and more, along with that milksop Beth, threatening my chance to get the hell out of school fifteen minutes early."

Mother laughs. She remembers all that too. Gone, thankfully, gone.

"In an instant, I push past Billy and run down the hall straight for the exit, where I hit the doors with a bang, releasing the bar, and spring out into the September afternoon. Bounding down the steps two at a time, I nearly barrel into a group of seniors smoking who call me an asshole, but I don't stop until I reach the far side of the playing field. I slide down the hill and the rest of the class comes tumbling after me, even Leslie, her blotchy freckles burning red and her legs smeared with grass stains.

Billy is triumphant. He raises his fist and dares Madame Forté to come out and wrap her prissy frog mouth around his Irish dick. Mark says she could stuff mille neuf cent soixante-quatorze up his ass. Funny, I don't remember Beth being there. And, it isn't long before the whole thing seems stupid. The bell rings, and the rest of the school spills out. I can see Madame Forté getting in her car. I have to go back, get my stuff from my locker. There is no more danger, no excitement, and Billy, who I had wanted to kiss, now seems a jerk, repeating over and over the few French swear words he had managed to learn. I trail back across the empty playing field and re-enter the school."

"You never told me this story?"

"I tried to never tell you anything, mother."

"What about the guy who was interviewing you?"

"Are you kidding, Frances? When I heard he was married to Beth, I freaked out and left. Walked right out onto the beach. I had to get away from him. Especially with that whole fucking day now rearing up in my head."

"Why what else happened?"

"Everything! Not many people can pinpoint the moment they lose their mind, but I can."

"No doubt this will involve me."

"Not necessarily, Mother. But as a Mother, and as you

in particular, you'll want some of the blame to fall at your feet."

"Fair enough."

"Will you two quit it. I want to hear the rest."

"Sorry." Mother and I can banter on endlessly in this vain much to the annoyance of Frances. "The beginning of my madness, starts at my locker. I can hear the faint ominous echo-y sounds and the receding shouts of my friends, and it makes me feel uneasy. Empty hallways are freaky enough, but it was more than that. I slam close my locker and head down the stairs. It is then that I hear the school superintendent, Mr. Rexall, a flint-hard man, who everybody said had once been caught jerking off in the girl's bathroom. He is coming up behind me with his tell-tale heavy jangle of keys. I would have taken off like a bat out of hell if I hadn't noticed through the doors leading to the first floor, Leslie, at her locker, struggling to get all her books in her backpack.

She is pretty surprised when she finds herself being dragged, my fingers sinking into her soft flesh, towards the exit. Two contrary forces never meant to be brought together, and we are acutely aware, in the most elemental way, of each other's physical presence, and, once out of doors, we spring apart as though by merely touching we have violated a law of nature. Even so, we fall into step because, what the fuck, we are heading in the same direction..."

"Are we still talking about Beth?"

"No, Mother. We're talking about Leslie."

"Leslie?"

"Lena's sister?"

"Oh that dreadful child. Ceaselessly polite. Difficult to look at."

"Mother!"

"I don't remember her at all, not really."

"Sometimes she's clearer in my mind than Lena. But not Heather."

I can see Mother shift. I can never tell what hearing Heather's name does to her, what it stirs up. If anything.

"Heather, who, as we round the corner, is sitting on the stone balustrade of their building.

'She must have forgotten her key,' Leslie whispers to me.

Heather gets up when she sees us.

'Mr. Rexall was roaming the halls,' I say.

'What would he want with you two?'

'Nothing. I didn't even see him,' Leslie says.

'So he was a figment of your imagination then?'

'I heard his keys.' I say. I could have killed Leslie, who by now is edging around us to head inside.

Heather sits back down on the balustrade, stretches out, lights a cigarette, and exhales a plume of blue smoke.

'The janitor,' she says, 'wasn't coming down the stairs so he could look at your baby boobs. Not that you would know what to do with him if he was. There's a room in the basement. That's where he fucks. And there are others. Men. Men so big they would rip you in two.'"

"Wait! There was a place like that?"

"Frances? A room where men fuck children in a high school? But whether there was or wasn't, my terror is absolute. Beneath the thin fabric of my top are my nipples, scratched raw in the inferno of adolescent growth and covered now by two band-aids. While Heather goes deeper into the details of the boiler room antics: mattresses thrown down; boys and girls, splayed and used, aroused and indifferent; men corrupting yet tender, netherworld of nether regions, only to re-emerge back upstairs and sit in class, the secret, swollen hurt making it hard to concentrate, I am fixated on my tits. You can go mad, Frances. In a second. It happened to me. By the time I get away from Heather and cross the park I was no longer safely moored to my mind. Heather's thrown-down mattress, the sheer violence of her thoughts as she coolly sat on the balustrade, her long-ago lifted skirt, the crisp ordinariness of that September afternoon, the sight of our stairs, my itchy boobs, my hands coming up to my face, then down again when blocking out the world did nothing at all. It seemed impossible that I would get home, climb the stairs, open a can of beans and butter toast.

Now I can unravel my thoughts, now on the other side of the world, and with forty years on my side. But then I was knocked flat, afraid as I was, I knew this was just the first note, a clang, a boom, off-key and crazy, but what was to follow would be worse and never-ending."

Frances gives a slight roll of the eye. She thinks my madness' are mad.

"Ok, maybe a little over the top. But I did feel this rage wash over me. Not directed at Heather but Lena. How could she not have warned me? Why hadn't she screamed us all into seeing what Heather was?"

"But you were the one with the knife."

"What, Mum?" Frances turns.

"Augati. Appearing by my bed at night with a knife in

hand. I don't think she knew whether to stab herself or me. I can hardly blame her. After my father. It was due to crop up again. But make up your bloody mind."

"Now it seems obvious I should have stabbed you, would have saved me a lot of bother."

Mother smiles.

"But you were unnerved enough to drag me to a shrink."

"You took Augati to a psychiatrist?"

"Dragged me there and dragged me out when that particular doctor told me that my panic and anxiety was no different than a little kid thinking there was a monster hiding under their bed. All I had to do was look and see I was safe."

"She cost me a fortune. All the Montreal models went to see her."

"Funny thing is, it was you that helped me in the end"

"Did I?"

"You were pretty fed up with me at this point."

"Where was Dad?" Frances asks.

"Yeah, where was he?"

"Either shacked up with some woman or working to all hours driving his business into the ground. But you were strategic, Aug, never wielding a knife when your father was around. It's him you should have been stabbing."

"Did he know that I thought I was going crazy?"

"Bits. But he was worried about Lena. Who, incidentally, was seeing a shrink too."

"She was!"

"Miles made me swear never to breathe a word of it. Liv felt that she was becoming to, what's the word, unto herself…"

"Introverted." Frances offers.

"No, something else. Detached."

"That fucking word again."

"'Tis awful. I would say, sullen. All you kids were. Vast gangs of sullen teenagers roaming the landscape until it was time for dinner. Is that what I told you? To stop being such a misery?"

"No. But one night after I yet again appeared with a knife, you got up and we went to sit in the living room. 'What,' you said, 'do you think this whole business of being alive is about?' I had no answer. That didn't stop you, 'Besides,' you said, 'getting up in the morning, dressing yourself, remembering to zip your zipper and button your buttons; besides writing one's column and remembering to put petrol in the car; besides finding time to read a book and, having a much-needed drink in the evening; besides cooking dinner and eating it, the only other job of being a human is to survive and half of survival, I would say in this modern life, most of survival is keeping one's brain in check. I could go mad, Augati. I could look at the pattern on that couch and let it swirl around in my brain until it meant something more until its very existence drew me past meaning into madness. Don't you think there haven't been times when I look around and think, who the hell am I? Everybody does. It's not madness; it's being human. And, that's hard. Very hard. But you have no choice. And I tell you another thing, my girl, while you may not think it, you have strength, inner reserves.'

"You said that Aug should survive by getting up and writing a column? Good one, Ma. Though, I am impressed, it's more advice than you ever given me."

"If I remember correctly, I was merely trying to get her to understand that I knew madness. My father went mad, died, as you know, in the insane asylum. I felt then that she was being…"

"Indulgent?" Frances says.

"Unthinking. When I was a teenager, rather than listening to the ticking of my brain, I had to deal with my poor old father."

"Must we? Mother?" Frances nudges her. The story is too old.

"He was such a great bear of a man. Hustling us down to the cold cellar when the bombing raids began. He'd throw this greatcoat over us. It stank. Meanwhile, he'd be mewling, crying out, telling us we're all going to perish. It's hardly the thing one wants to hear. I hated him. But then, I didn't realise, none of us did, was that with each raid his brain was giving way a little bit more, until…"

"He went bonkers, we know."

"Not at first, Frances. At first, he sat by the window days on end, head in hand. That used to infuriate my mother. She was never one for sitting around. Then, as the nightly raids grew worse, whole blocks were being wiped out, he took to standing in the middle of the street just staring up at the mayhem raining down. It got out of control when, when, well, he started to strip off his clothes. We wouldn't have known if the family across the way hadn't fled when their roof caved in. Out they rushed to the sight of my naked father. They came for him, not that day, but soon after. By then, he was quite insane. Had visions of grandeur, not even visions, since he was convinced that he was a Lord or a Duke. For the rest of the war, once a month we took a bus, its route often changed because of various streets being obliterated. Sometimes it would take hours to get to the hospital. It was horrible sitting there having tea with him; his huge Russian head pitched forward. I don't know why we bothered. He didn't know who we were. And then he died."

"I wonder what he would have been diagnosed with now? I don't think "insane" is allowed anymore." I say.

"Is gassed? Or is that wiped from history too?"

"Gassed? Is that what you think happened?"

"Gas, what's that?"

"Mustard, Frances darling, Mustard gas. All over France during the first world war. He was gassed, and it mucked up his brain."

"What? And, it took twenty years to manifest itself?"

"You're one to talk, Augati," Frances says, struggling to get off the couch. She needs another cup of coffee and Mother another cup of tea. Left holding the computer, Mother lets it slide; my view now is a pillow and a dog's nose.

"There was one doctor who helped?" I say.

"Who?"

My view is even more obscure, the computer now on the floor.

"Mother!"

A dog's rush, Frances hands, a seasick moment, but we are all settled again until the kettle boils.

"That old man."

"Oh yes,"

"Who are you talking about?"

"Mother found him, or he found us, something. This strange old man, a healer of sorts, was he even a doctor?"

"I'm not sure. But I found him."

"Remember how nervous we were? That preserved brown room, all polished wood, and creaky floorboards. There were books, bound, with the titles engraved. From the shadows came an ancient man, marooned in a worn cardigan. His touch was papyrus. I wanted him to hold my hand forever.

He had no interest in the fact that I had been showing at your bedroom door with a knife. He wanted to know all about…"

"That's right! That you were born dead."

"You were born dead?"

"A blue baby. Not entirely blue, but blue enough, until she snapped into life. Then she was spectacularly red with her eczema."

"Haven't had that in years."

"Always bloody scratching. Drove me mad, behind your knees, the crooks of your arms."

"Worse was my eyelids." I close my eyes. "I think it is all scar tissue."

I open them, Frances fills the screen.

"Hard to tell." she peers, then pulls back.

Mother reappears. "Your blueness did upset him, but it was your father that enraged him."

"That's par for the course."

"What did Daddy do?"

"He said, 'We didn't come down from the trees to have a child perpetually clamped to the breast.' He wanted them milk-free and on-call."

"But, you breastfed me."

"My tits were no longer required."

Once again, can we blame our parents for everything?

"How did Aug eat?"

"She didn't. At first. Rejected formula outright. We had to stay in the bloody hospital until she saw fit to like the stuff."

"That's why that tiny old man rose like a mad king, his finger in your face, and said, 'You've been killing your daughter since birth!'"

"I should have swotted him away, like a fly."

"You say that now, but you were scared shitless."

The kettle is screaming. Frances gets up again. "Don't say anything until I get back." Again the computer slides onto the couch, no dog this time. I can hear Mother telling Frances she wants extra sugar in her tea. What was that doctor's name? He gave me a bottle of white powder; I carried it with me for years. Probably a placebo, it fizzed in water. But, I believed, and it calmed me.

I hear the cups being put on the coffee table, and my view is righted again.

"What was mother killing you with?"

"Cows"

"Cows?"

"Apparently, ruminants are full of enzymes, and they can fuck with your hormones, and when you are an adolescent, there are plenty of hormones to fuck with."

"Enzymes? Like Oxi-clean?"

"I wondered that. I don't know."

"I had just done a bloody big shop. You were always complaining that there was not enough food in the house. I'd be buggered if I was now going to waste it all. But Lena, she insisted. Said there was no way you'd have enough discipline to resist cheese and pickle sandwiches, ice cream, Tortiere pie. I told her then she should take the food to her mother, but…"

Mother stops. I've seen this. I know it. The weight of memory. All those years fearing what Lena might be dragging back to her house, the fights between her and Miles, the state of the bathtub, the calcified cat shit under the couch, dishes piled in the sink, laundry folded then left on the kitchen table, the splatter-dash rug, the walls grimed by children's handprints, Frances forgotten; in the car, on the stairs, in her jolly jumper, the dead plants, the slimed humidifier, the greyish sheets, stale bread, rancid butter, furry ice cream, laddered pantyhose, empty vodka bottles, the dirty windows, but the thought of those things being known to Liv, didn't hurt as much as the two of us standing in that shabby kitchen, both of us pricked by embarrassment, as Lena told us that Piers wouldn't want our food in his house.

"Never mind, darling. We just threw it out." Mum says, not looking at me.

"Aug eats cheese now."

"And hamburgers. I grew. My brain grew. Or, I am willing to poison myself. I'm poisoning myself staying up this late. I need sleep."

"What time is it there?"

"After two."

"C's still up?"

"God, no."

Mother leans in. "It is night there?"

"It is."

I've been disconnected before I have a chance to say good-night. Mother must have inadvertently pressed a button.

I couldn't find the carrots. They had moved them again. It is now onions in that bin. Tomorrow, something else. The carrots were over by the tomatoes, which were the beets yesterday. All I wanted was a few things. But I haven't learned. This world, one awash in workers, can't let anything stay put. The carrots, the pickles, the tofu, the cheese, the chips, the cookies, the washing-up liquid, the toilet paper, all of it, nightly, put on a forced march so that I'm left spinning in circles. What was, is no longer. Once I found the carrots, they didn't speak to me. Neither did the eggplant or the potatoes. I picked up a package of corn. Real, yellow, firm corn from Australia. It's ridiculous I had to come to the Middle East to find corn so much better than the pale, candified mealy ears that pass as corn in the States these days. But nothing coalesced around them either.

Preparing supper is the most hopeful thing a person can do. There have been times when I have been saved by the simple act of putting something in the oven, that particular leap of faith that in an hour a beautiful roast chicken will emerge or a lovely rack of lamb. I stayed, willing an idea. Finally, the tomatoes spoke. They are roasting now. I'll make a simple sauce with homemade pasta and tonight C, and I will sit and eat and try not to think about tomorrow.

I will answer the emails I got this morning from friends asking what my address is. "I want to send you a Christmas card." In truth, there are only a few who persist. Christmas cards being one of those tit for tat exchanges. I've never sent one.

What do these people think? I'm in Cincinnati? That they can send a card out and it will get to me in two days?

We have no address, not one that would make sense to a card sent from America. Somewhere is a P.O. box, we've certainly been asked for it enough times on various forms, but its whereabouts is still a mystery. But the markers of a life: zip code and street name? Those don't exist. At least not where I live. Keep your cards and save your postage.

Do the streets skirting this complex even have names? I've come to the window. There are no street signs. If it is named, it won't be for long. Everything here is recast, renamed, reborn. Giving directions to cab drivers is slapstick. "Near the old Monte Carlo club, around the corner from the new hotel, the one not completed, just passed the ground they are digging for the Mosque, then do a u-turn."

U-turns. There's a malevolent, capricious traffic god out there taking a sinister delight as one sails miles past their destination before being allowed to make a U-turn. We fightback by driving at breakneck speeds. Something the government is trying to curtail by showing before movies the most horrific images of mangled cars and their newly expired occupants.

I should do some Christmas shopping. Notebooks for C. I don't need anything. After buying all the stuff for this place, I don't have the stomach for shopping. If anything, a new mascara? Lena was the one who liked giving presents. Mother certainly never did, lazily wrapping gifts in newspaper, leaving the price tag on, reading the book first, so the spine was broken, the pages stained. But Lena knew how to do presents, wrapped them in pretty paper, included a card on which she wrote in her tiny script: Love from your sister, Lena. I think of her gifts as often as I think of her knitting. Her fingers alive, quick, exact. Mother knit too. But with her, it was more of a tousle, a wild ride with her needles so big that whatever she was knitting was loose, misshapen. On purpose, of course. Lena's sweaters, mittens, caps, dickies, tea cozies, were geometric and required a lot of counting of stitches, of knit one, purl one, of casting off and casting on. Four thin needles at a go for a sleeve or a band for a hat. Her knitting bag was full of softball-size tightly bound balls of wool, or cotton. She liked to knit cotton sweaters. She said that sometimes handling wool for hours on end made her hands feel like they were full of a weird animal energy, or the opposite as if the yarn was sucking all the moisture and blood from her. I remember her trying to tell me how it felt after an hour or two of deep concentration. "It's a conversation Aug, but I'm not the speaker." I didn't know what she meant, still, don't since I can't knit or sew at all.

You would have thought Mother and Lena would have come together over their knitting. Perhaps not. Mother whined about her struggles with her thick needles, and the chasm between her initial concept and the final creation, never though did she undo a miscounted line.

Lena never complained. Sensing one extra stitch, she would unravel hours worth of work. Mother's sweaters were lopsided. Lena's never were. The Bayeux tapestry. You marvel. You think of the work. But you don't want to tear it from the wall and wrap the Battle of Hastings around your shoulders and snuggle down.

But when I was sitting with her while she knitted, I would fall into a trance, the rhythm, and light click of her needles, a natural hypnotic. I think now it might have been the only time I ever felt calm. It left something with me, a need for gentle repeating noise. I have a metronome or had, and for years I would set it on low and hope it would slow the riot in my mind. Anything she knitted as a gift was wrapped in paper, no box, so you always had a clue what it was — her only vanity.

The best sweater she ever made might have been her last. White cotton, sort of drappy, with navy blue striped pockets and a few thin navy stripes running horizontally. She was pleased with it, inordinately so. She planned to wear it at her first sailing meet. Sailing teams, riding camps, tennis clubs, these were all part of her other life. All paid for by Piers, the good businessman, who saw a Honda Civic at a trade show and saw the future. My father, the bad businessman, was grappling with the high cost of having to convert his old beauties so they met new emission standards. All his money was tied up in saving his cars, sending me to trot around on a quarter horse executing jumps was out of the question.

But that sweater didn't make it. It died on my fifteenth birthday.

As with every other birthday, regardless if you are also going to have a party, there is a family dinner with all your favourite foods. Spare ribs in my case, which, as Lena and I huddle in the bathroom, are sitting in butcher's paper, blood pooling, while Mother looks through the newspaper trying to decide which page will make the best wrapping paper for my birthday present. Frances is bathing her Barbie in a sink full of potato peelings. On my bed lays Mother's birthday poem, which she left by my head sometime in the night so that it will be there staring me in the face when I wake in the morning.

Super Augusta, or, to those in the know, super
Augati!

Let's trace the nights and say from your first to this
your fifteenth.

Mislaid, I'm afraid, the very moment of your birth
but not the circumstance...

As you tried to struggle out
And an intern
And a nurse
Discursed
On South Pacific
(one thought terrible,
the other, terrific)
Back and forth
They sent their argument
As I lay
wanting to say
Nurse! I think it's coming any minute!
And she said (but not to me)
They should have put Mary Martin in it...then sang
"...one enchanted evening
you may see a stranger
across a crowded room..."
And I, inwardly,
Cried
Nurse! Nurse!
You will see a stranger!
But from this thudding womb!

I found all my birthday poems when I was packing up
her stuff. Most glued together, a mass of my passing years,

her optimistic renderings of my future written in the margins of pictures cut out from magazines and pasted onto cardboard, none bearing any relation of my actual life. I had tossed most of them out, except the few I could salvage.

Lying in my room, smoking my joint, I hear Lena arrive, but nothing seems weird. Frances abandons her Barbie and runs down the hall to let her know that the cake hasn't been made yet. But Lena doesn't go into the kitchen to see if she can help. Instead, I hear the vacuum cleaner being run around the dining room table with a near-comical clatter of everything from lego bits to coins being sucked up. I hear her start to set the table, saw her frown as she tries to make sense of Mab's mismatched plates and wine glasses.

My father will be home, eventually. It is my birthday. The family hasn't become so frayed that birthdays can be ignored. Stoned, the muffled sounds coming from the rest of the flat lull me to sleep and I wake with a start to Lena standing in the doorway, gesturing for me to follow her. I get up, and we go into the bathroom where, without saying a word, she holds out her wrists. Each sports a large band-aid, even so, I can see, at the edges, the ends of a couple of cuts.

"Heather took my sweater," she says, "She took it, wore it, then pulled it apart and left it, a jumble on my pillow."

"What? What sweater?"

Lena pulled her sleeves down, "You know which one. I was going to burn it, something, but Mum came into the room. She saw it but said nothing. Then Leslie came in. She didn't say anything either. Instead, Mum got up on my desk and asked Leslie to hand up my former sweater. Cotton, wool too, when it's thoroughly tangled like that, it's helpful to have gravity working with you. She stood on my desk, letting it fall through her fingers while Leslie wound it. It didn't take long. When Heather came back, she looked at my pillow and said, 'If you re-knit that sweater, you should make the sleeves longer.' As if I would ever re-knit it."

"But, your wrists?"

Lena merely shakes her head, and clicks open the bathroom door.

"I have to iron some napkins,"

I know enough not to follow her. Lena has told me as much as she is willing to say. I go back to my room and ferret out my container of white powder. I haven't used it in a couple of years, but right now, I need to know, at least, exactly where it is.

There are a few gifts arrayed around my plate. My big present is a new bed. My old one has sprung so many springs it is next to impossible to sleep on. The ribs are cooked, the cake is made. Lena, when she realizes the nature of the meal, takes away the knives and forks and brings out finger bowls top with floating slices of lemon. My father dips his fingers into his bowl and carefully dries his hands each time before taking a swig of his drink. Mother lets her glass get smeared with the sticky residue of the ribs. I eat with René Lévesque's face staring up at me. The back of my head feels like it is in a vice grip, that grows tighter as I watch Lena's sleeves pull back each time she dips her fingers into her bowl. Frances, never patient, wants us to hurry up so I can open her present.

Finally, she can stand it no longer and goes around the table, taking up everyone's plates. She then hands me her present to be opened or rather unfurled, since her gift is a rolled-up piece of paper, tied with a ribbon.

I remember the heavy-weight of Frances pressing up against me as I untie the ribbon and slowly scroll open the page. At the top, in mother's hand, is written: STORY CONCEIVED BY FRANCES QUICK, DRAWN BY FRANCES QUICK, DICTATED BY FRANCES QUICK BUT WRITTEN OUT BY MAB QUICK.

Frances, needing to make sure that I follow the layout, points with a finger still sticky with rib sauce. "Each morning, she has short hair. But all she has to do is brush it, and her hair goes to any length she wants. See? There? That's for a party. So she brushed it really long. And there, it's a windy day, so she doesn't brush it much at all...."

"That's amazing."

"I know," Frances says. "And she could do important things with her hair. Like if a puppy was drowning, she could brush it quickly and send it out to him. But I didn't draw that part. Now, open Mummy's," Frances says, handing me René Lévesque's face. I tear it in two.

It is a book. I turn it over; it is *The Bell Jar* by Sylvia Plath.

Mother smiles at me. "To make you think, darling."

Lena reaches for the book.

"I thought about killing myself."

"Did you, darling?" My father's face wears what I think of as his mild expression: his eyes half-mast, his head tilted. It isn't keen interest, but it wasn't dismal either.

"This afternoon," Lena says, opening the book to read the jacket copy.

The terrible tightness that I have been feeling across the back of my head now is intolerable.

"See," Lena says, presenting one of her wrists.

Mother, when she sees the band-aid, gasps and buries her head in her hands. My father stands up.

"What in god's name were you thinking?" He knocks the book out of Lena's hands and takes hold of her wrists. "Let me see."

"There's nothing to see. I didn't do it right. I went across, and I didn't go very deep. I think I was testing myself."

"This is not something you bloody well play at."

"Everyone thinks about it," Lena says, pulling her sleeves down. "Most just don't do it."

Mother, having recovered somewhat, lunges across the table, "Give me that bloody book."

"Don't worry," Lena says, "I've read it already. And, I know that Plath stuck her head in the oven even though she was American."

"What difference does that make?" my father roars.

"I think what Lena is saying is that Americans will most likely shoot themselves or take pills," Mother says, "While it's entirely British to put your head in the oven. I think it has something to do with coal."

"Yes," Lena says, "The first time she tried to kill herself, she took pills."

Dad, still shaken, sits down. "This is unacceptable. There will be no pills and," he takes up Lena's arm again, "no other things."

I want to cry out, "You mean, no taking up razor blades and slicing your wrists?" Frances has started to whimper.

She doesn't understand what is happening other than that Lena's present has yet to be opened, and things aren't looking good for the chocolate birthday cake, which is still unfrosted. No candles. No song. The party, as far as she can tell, is a bust.

I don't remember who suggests that Lena should come and live with us for her own safety, if nothing else. If it was mother, then, well, how can my father leave if his favourite daughter is living under his roof? The fact that for the entire marriage, she has done her best to prevent the very thing from happening, fearing being constantly shown up and marginalized by her stepdaughter must have run through her mind. But it is mother who leads Lena to the back room, a room off the kitchen that never served any purpose, other than to be empty, cold, and dark. Over the years, various uses for it had been attempted. In a fit of trying to be something she would never be, Mother had set up a sewing nook complete with her dressmaker's form, whose original exact curves were now completely bent out of shape. But the one window offered no direct light so she couldn't see to sew. We then tried to make it a playroom for Frances. My father had even painted a blackboard on the wall, but she never played in there. And recently, Mother had tried to make it less of an eyesore by starting a wall collage of torn-out magazine and art book pictures, but she soon got bored, leaving behind a still open and long-ago congealed can of rubber cement. I have, as one of my reoccurring dreams, a nightmare about a house with an extra room wherein resides pure evil. It must be based on that room, which didn't even allow privacy since my father had cut a hole

in the wall years before. And, now here she is offering it
to Lena.

Heather is not mentioned.

After that Lena and my father drive over to her house. I
imagine my father's dislike of Piers would have made him
brusque. "I have decided Lena should live with me for the
time being."

No doubt Piers would have started to protest since he
didn't know about the sweater or about Heather sticking
her cunt in my father's face, or that she, even if only in
her mind, spent her days down in the school basement
being fucked by older men. He didn't know either that
under her bed she had stowed so many stolen objects,
most of them worthless but some not, that Liv, ignoring
her unease at the sight of the pilfered stuff, including her
Chanel skirt and a rope of pearls, didn't even attempt to
vacuum. It was the only un-vacuumed part of the house.
Piers standing in the doorway saw no reason to contain
his acquisitive impulse to grab his stepdaughter and close
the door. But then he felt Liv take his hand and give it
a hard squeeze. For whatever reasons, ones he couldn't
even begin to fathom, Lena is to be allowed to leave.

While they are gone, I smoke another joint and
eventually take a peek at *The Bell Jar.*

I brought it, didn't I? It's packed in one of the boxes
still stacked in the guest-less guest room.

Yes, here it is. I used to stare into the rings on the
cover, psyching myself out. "Let your' madness' lead to
creativity. Love and Kisses, Mum."

I had forgotten Plath starts right off with the
Rosenbergs. There was never any threat of Heather being

fried. The electric chair was as American as killing oneself with pills or guns.

I should unpack these boxes. But there comes a point when putting one more thing away, on a shelf, in a drawer, is impossible. And, somehow, seeing these boxes each time I come into the guest room reminds me that this is not home no matter how many pictures I put up or how many times I walk the dogs around the complex. A rootless city, literally and figuratively.

When Lena starts living with us, everything changes. The lint is removed from the dryer. Old cartons of milk are thrown out. Washing is folded and put away. One day I came home to find the bathtub full of bleach as if anything could scare away the decades-old stains that had seeped into the porcelain. She rotates the towels, makes sure the sugar bowl is full and not clumpy. Her morning alarm can be heard through the flat. Before, we all relied on Mother, who claims that anyone born on the docks is a lifetime early riser. Frances' pigtails are even and, at least, to my mind look painful. Lost socks are thrown out, not left in a basket hoping one day to find another mate. There is less yelling, less door slamming because Frances, with a patient sister like Lena, isn't always trying to get into my room. Our closeness wasn't always in the cards. Frances could harbour a mountain of resentment and hurt for all the times I told her to "Fuck off and leave me alone." Lena is willing to read her books, play Barbie, the door to her room is open when she is home. Remembering this, it all sounds so lovely, but it created this terrible unease, our lives were thrown out of balance, or perhaps for the first time balanced, which can create its own sense of vertigo.

My father having made his presence felt the first few weeks starts to fade away again. Mother, with pursed lips, will tell Lena, "No, he's not expected home for dinner." Did Lena at these moments feel a stranger in a strange home?

Once at school, I see her sitting on the steps with Leslie; they have their heads together and are holding hands. I feel sick knowing that the sympathy is for Lena, who has to deal daily with the unending squalor of our house, deal with my moods, Frances' rambunctiousness, Mother's work.

Now I think I was wrong. Lena was reaching out to assure Leslie that, while she may not be living with her, she still wanted to offer some protection against Heather. But back then, I would never have imagined that Leslie, with her sloping shoulders, wandering eye, lacklustre hair could be in the orb of Heather's twisted interest. Lena is another story. She is beautiful, not like Heather, not eerie and other-worldly, but somehow her sadness has burnished her with her grave blue eyes, long lashes, trim figure. Always a solitary, people nonetheless gravitate towards her. She helps, listens, but rarely laughs.

Heather is around. I must pass her in the hallways between periods a million times. But, and I guess this is true of the students here on this small campus, caught in your slipstream, you flow passed without a sideways glance. I suspect though by now, kids have started to sniff out that there is something pitched not right about her. Her beauty is off-putting; it allows no one in; there is no shared experience. If she is having a cigarette with a bunch of other girls, she stands in the middle, ringed.

There are rumours that she is fucking older men and that she might have fucked Billy Underhill's big brother Seamus, whippet-thin but handsome in that scorned Irish way. The older men, maybe, but Seamus? Not unless there is some cruel, sadistic undercurrent to it.

One day coming home from school, I see Heather sitting on our steps. She merely stands and nods her head. How she knew no one was home, I have no idea.

I follow her up the stairs, which, as always, are strewn with boots, skis, skates, old milk bottles. She kicks aside a cross-country ski. It clatters down.

Inside the flat, Heather walks right over to a wall of photos, black and whites, taken by my father. He had a darkroom rigged up until Mother wandered in one time too many, and he smashed the enlarger to the ground. The line of pictures stops at Frances as a baby. Lena around thirteen. And me nearing twelve.

"What's that?"

"Lena. Halloween."

"What is she supposed to be?"

"A cat."

Heather leans in. Lena in a cat costume: black tights with a tail sewn on, whiskers painted on her face. I had the idea of weaving a bent coat hanger across her head through her braids to make ears. It didn't work. They kept flopping down. It was the first and only time the two of us went Trick-or-Treating together. Lena wanted to be a cat because Liv insisted each Halloween that the three girls dress up in some national costume. Feline was a radical step. I can't remember what I was, probably an Indian princess; we had to do something with all those Indian bedspreads.

Heather turns away from the pictures and goes into my parent's bedroom. The bed unmade, the sheets grey, and Frances' toys all over the place. She lays down, stretching her limbs to all four corners. I have a terrible urge to grab the comforter and stuff as much as I can into my mouth.

"How do you think my father feels knowing that your father fucked Liv first?" she asks, rolling off the bed, opening mother's closet and starting to rifle through her clothes. Is she scouring for another skirt whose hem she could lift to expose herself yet again to my father? When she stops at mother's blue jersey skirt, I say, "That one is covered in cat piss."

Heather lets go of the skirt. "Show me Lena's room."

The door that had been the coffee table reconstituted into a door again so Lena can have some privacy doesn't fit properly in the jamb. To enter, you throw your weight. The room is dark, neat as a pin.

"The maid's quarters?"

Maid's quarters? That had never occurred to any of us.

Ten minutes later, the room doesn't matter. Not with the house reverberating with the sound of the slammed front door. Not with the pressure, I can still feel between my legs.

Had I not followed Heather into the living room, had I not also plopped myself down at the other end of our large couch, then there would have been no chance for her to extend her foot into my crotch, leaving it there, firm but without applying any extra pressure. But I had followed her, and once she had me pinned, I didn't dare move.

I never speak of that moment, not even to C. It is too small. Meaningless. In the scheme of things. But the scheme of things hadn't happened yet when she put her foot in my crotch and surrounded by these boxes, by things packed away, it is impossible not to feel every second of those seconds, the silence after she left, the fear that I might be aroused.

That night I wake thinking; she's taken something. But what? Not mother's skirt, or any of her clothes. I had checked after hearing the front door slam. But I know Heather has taken something. Then it hits me. The air! She has taken the air. The night is empty, a vacuum, and we are going to die. I sit up. I need to wake everyone. But there is no light. Heather has taken that as well. Running from the room, I stumble and fall.

Mother understands instantly that there is no air. She turns and shakes my father, who gets up without question and heads towards Lena's room while Mother goes to Frances, who fusses at being woken in the middle of the night. My father leads us all downstairs, out into the night. I am surprised to see the street lamps burning. I keep my eye on the faint glow. My father looks back up at the house.

"What did you say you smelt? Gas?"

The flat, my room, is being raked by the Place Ville Marie light. Where had that been? I know of space, of black holes, of points in the universe so dense that no light, with it's weak, bendable properties, could nudge its way in. But this is different, Lena has stolen the air.

"Gas, did you smell gas?" Mother nudges me.

I don't know how to answer. It isn't something; it is nothing. Finally, I say, "There was no air."

"No air?" My father, the former RAF pilot. He knows

thin air. He knows air sucked out from one's lungs by G-force. He knows panicked breaths brought on by losing altitude, hurtling down, down towards the ground, your plane unresponsive, your controls lax. But no air? What was no air?

"Like space," I say.

"Your daughter had another one of her nightmares."

"Bloody hell, Aug." Mother winces, Frances is driving her head painfully into her shoulder.

"It wasn't a nightmare."

Everyone starts back up the stairs. I have no choice but to follow. It is only once inside that I notice the picture of Lena as a cat is missing.

"I found it when I went to bed," Lena says, coming up behind me, "It was smashed, slashed, and hidden under my sheets."

Later that night, I crawl into her bed even though I know she doesn't want me sleeping with her; still, I am not kick out. And, in the morning, I wake to find she is holding my hand.

Or was she? Have I changed history, memory? It doesn't seem like Lena.

I should either unpack these boxes or throw all this shit out. C phoned. He's going to come home early. The campus, empty because of the winter break, is starting to depress him.

Oh, I had forgotten I had packed this envelope of old copies of mother's columns, the few I saved. I was going to do a book incorporating her columns. Before we left Brooklyn, I was full of ideas. I might attempt a podcast. I was going to run a writing workshop for women over forty. Now, I don't want to do anything.

Sing a song of singles
Give me a life that's free
Goodbye to being his better half
I'm keeping it all for me!

That's what you think. Or, that's what I thought. But a single parent is not a single. Not by a long shot. Singles can watch the T.V. program of their choice. Singles don't have to stock peanut butter, pop tarts, and other easy-eat child fodder. Singles need nothing more fattening in the fridge than crab meat. Singles can give themselves an asparagus-whip facial without providing a spectacle for jeering kids. Singles don't have to go to "For All" movies. Singles can fly to Boston for tea parties.

At least when I was married, I was a couple. Now I seem to have multiplied. With my daughters, I'm a triple. First reports of my status as a threesome were confused. Word got out that I was running a "ménage a trois," and there was a flurry of excitement, but it quickly subsided when it became apparent who the other two were. Not that I didn't expect the flavour of our lives to change once the three of us were alone.

I had to save this one; it should have been the only one. These others, they can go, even if I have brought them so far.

Mother still sports a couple of bruises when she wrote this. She calls me into her office to read it to me. I'm now her listener, since Daddy has moved out leaving behind all his clothes and Lena. She is not in the column.

Not a month before she had finally witnessed one of my parent's fights, the worst and, as it happened, the last.

As Miles and Mab battle it out, Lena, Frances, and I huddle in my bedroom. The early violence is mostly reflective, as Mother repeatedly charges my father like a battering ram, and he strives to keep her off. If he is going to leave, she needs to feel it. But then something changes, he snaps, his blows now are meant to convey an absolute end. Playacting is over, as is the marriage.

When mother appears, shaken, her bruises and swelling starting to raise, we hear behind her the final front door slam. Frances has buried her head in my lap and is reluctant to let go. It is Lena who gets up and hugs her. Mother, probably for the first time ever, collapses into her boney embrace. It is also Lena who, when my father unexpectedly returns, stands beside him with her hand on his back. He has come back because he wants to make it clear to us that this time, he is leaving for good.

"It is all," he said, looking vaguely around my room and never at my mother. "impossible."

But as I listen to mother read, occasionally stopping to tweak a sentence, I daren't say, "We are not three, we are four."

But this column, pounded out in a fury, is her declaration. Those who don't know will now know. Miles has left her. But she is funny, so fuck him.

When we split, my husband and I shared a mutual belief that each stood in the other's way to self-realization. I'm not entirely sure what he was after, but it was certainly a glossier life than the one we were leading. And one marked by the persistent image of me with shopping bags and smudges of Miss Clairol hair dye on my ear tips was seriously disruptive to it.

And, of course, as I saw it, he was the one who was inhibiting me from vegetarianism, coming to grips with Jung and on-the-spot crusading. Especially on-the-spot crusading. The notion of just sending donations and wearing buttons seems limp and, well, housebound. I want to be out there where the action is like Vanessa or Jane. I have made attempts, but the children are proving to be major stumbling blocks. I can never convince them that a protest meeting is an outing and a treat. Not that I didn't expect the flavour of our lives to change once the three of us were alone. I honestly looked forward to moving little scenes with Augati and Frances stoutly declaring: "It's just us now, mummy." I saw them becoming sunny, positive creatures who never gave me a moment's trouble or played Elton John pitched at volumes to dismantle my nervous system. But the bitter truth is they haven't changed. They still get cracker crumbs on the couch and continue to be a mixture of nice and nasty, naughty and good.

I sense an editor's touch with that ending. And, if mother hopes excluding Lena will be a subtle clue that perhaps she should pack her bags and leave, well, it is missed by Lena. Mother stews, drops asides, is mean, Lena stays on. Until one night, she asks her if she likes living with us.

"Not really," she says, "But..."

Mother ignores the "but" and says, "Then it would be best for everyone if you go back home." I say nothing, and if there is any direct guilt that I harbour, it lies in this moment. But so much wasn't said or asked. Where was my father? I mean, I know where he was, he had taken a small flat on Sherbrooke Street, of which all I remember was it had bay windows and a locked closet where, I presume, his mistress (not the one that bought the couch, another one just as mysterious) stashed her stuff. He had left all of us, but Lena more. Why didn't he take responsibility for her? I do not doubt that I would have been hurt and more than a little jealous if he had taken her to live with him. But he should have been in on the decision and the fact that he wasn't, makes him culpable. Mother too, perhaps even more so, she knew, we all knew at this point that Heather was unstable. Although to be fair, you don't think, you never can imagine. And, Lena gave no indication that going back would be any worse than living with us. At least, in her other home, the rules made sense, the rhythm of the days better suited her.

I have no memory of her moving out, packing her clothes and books, only that the empty room doesn't seem any emptier for having been occupied.

Over the summer, I hardly see her. Once or twice at Daddy's when Frances and I visit him. She is still part of the sailing team and is at their lake house most the of time. Nobody goes to our land anymore, and won't until years later when I mention to C that my family has an old abandoned cabin in the woods of Quebec. A day later, we are driving north. He inhabits the place, loves the wreck of it all, the wild beauty, the pond, the building fires, the cold nights. I would, too, if...

Come fall, mother busy, I have to take Frances to

get her new shoes for school. We go to Moe's shoe shop on Greene Avenue. Moe's has a new sign which sports a freshly painted apostrophe. Among many of the latest edicts being handed down by the newly installed Separatist government, no apostrophes. And, all business transactions henceforth are to be conducted in French as well. But, as we entered Moe's, we hear nothing but determined English. Frances wants red Buster Brown's. As always. The place is packed with harried mothers trying to get their children to stand still so their ever-growing feet can be measured. A few look up and whisper when they realize we are Mab Quick's children. Moe comes to our aid and tries to hide his impatience as Frances walks up and down the store, not once but three times testing her new shoes. After she deems them perfect, Moe snatches them off her feet and roughly stuffs them back in the box. At the cash, Frances is close to tears so, before crossing the street to the stationery store for my school supplies, I let her repack them neatly.

Frances chooses to wait by the erasers so she can smell them as I collect all the stuff I need, a geometry set, pencil case, Wite-out, a couple of vetted erasers, a ruler, and some spiral notebooks. While paying, at the last second, I pick up a super ball for her.

We walk home along Sherbrooke Street under banners hanging from balconies proclaiming the owner's intent to either stay or leave. The leavers seem to have the upper hand. But like all our friends who swore they would forsake America and never return if Donald Trump got elected, I doubt any of my neighbours left either.

Frances, who insists on carrying her shoes, has fallen

so far behind that I sit down at a bus stop to wait for her. A bus pulls up, the doors heave open and stand agape. I can see an old woman working her way up the aisle. My eyes drift along the length of the bus. A girl is staring at me without expression but certainly not blank. It is Lena.

Time holds us.

The old lady climbs down, the door hisses close, and the bus moves forward, taking Lena with it. The spell is broken. Frances comes up beside me.

"Did you see that?"

"What?"

"Lena was on the bus."

"Our Lena?"

"She just stared at me. Said nothing."

Frances looks at the receding bus, and then, in one fluid move, she hurls her super ball hard after it, and we watch as its ever-diminishing trajectory fails to catch up.

It is not the hour. The hour? As if that mattered. But it is dark, and C is asleep. I've come out into the living room where the spotlight from the massive hotel they are building on the beach shines into the room. The work goes on 24/7, but it never seems more complete. Perhaps watching a building being built is like aging; one day, there is a wrinkle, but you don't notice it forming, and from then on, that's it, it's part of the aged you.

This is my vigil, one I have to do alone — the remembering of the night. Yesterday, I rooted out from the bottom of yet another box the cassette tape of Mother's storm broadcast. I had packed it but forgot a cassette player. I called C near tears, though truth be told, I could probably recite every word. He scoured the university and found an old Walkman.

I always start by trying to imagine where all the players are now. I'm here. Frances in L.A. will be thinking about getting some lunch. Mother is sitting in her chair, bent over a crossword, her last connection to words, and they are still an abiding puzzle. My father lies in his grave. And Lena? I place her too. Like me, on the cusp of the horror ready to make the once yearly leap.

Then.

I am in class. I had left the house with wet hair, and for those first few minutes, my hair hangs in frozen tendrils. Outside it is snowing, hard. A blizzard, having moved in far quicker than they had predicted, is why we are in school; no snow warning had been issued. It is the last day before the Christmas break. I have not done my homework. I have a scratch on my face. Frances wouldn't put her foot in her snow boot; I pinched her, she scratched me.

Frances, dropped off by me, is playing down in the basement of her school with kids of other orphaned classes because several teachers, who had to come in from the suburbs, had seen the writing on the wall and had turned around fearing they would get stuck in the city.

Mother, summoned in by her producer, arrives at C.B.C as crews are getting ready to go out and cover the storm, which is now being called "Storm of the Century."

My father is in town. He has come in to finalize the selling of his business to Piers. I don't know about this, nor does Mother. We thought he had come in from Ottawa to spend Christmas with us. As Mother is being asked by her producer to write something funny that would take all of our minds off the storm, my father is screwing a former mistress of his until he has to meet Piers, and Billy Underhill is kicking the back of my chair so he can show me a mammoth joint he has rolled.

Liv is at home, where along the hallway, five sets of skis are lined up with their boots and poles. Piers, before he left for work, had told her the ski trip was off and that it was Miles Quick's fault. His business isn't worth two nickels rubbed together, so Piers wouldn't be getting the windfall he expected from the planned resale. He was going to meet with Miles that afternoon and tell him the whole deal was off. Liv knows she should be putting the skis away; instead, she is laying out cups for the girls for when they come home from school, and she will make them hot chocolate. She can't pretend she was never married to Miles; there is Lena, after all. Nor, in all these years, is she able to shake the guilt.

Lena and Leslie are also in class, just down the hall.

Having them close now seems familiar. In art class, I am hardly aware of Leslie as she sits bent over her drawings. And Lena and I like to momentarily link fingers when we pass each other in the hallway.

I can't see Heather. Her movements are forever murky until she flashes into vivid form.

My teacher is losing patience with me. I have not done the reading, but I do not care. It is barometric. Water-borne bodies subjected to influences far (the tidal pull of the moon) and wide (polar vibrations, weather fronts, air pressure). Not that my teacher isn't hostage to the same forces, the full moon, the same massive ridge of low pressure that is bringing with it the storm. She resents that she doesn't get to mumble and stare off, doesn't get to examine her nails, chew on the ends of her hair, nor does she, like half the boys in class, get to sit, hands down her pants, half asleep.

But before she can yell at me, or give me extra work to do over the break, the principal enters the room. He is grave and officious. The storm has intensified, changed course, and moved in faster than anyone expected. All schools are being let out early, and, with stern warnings, he tells us that everyone should head straight home. Phones in both the common room and the school office will be available if anyone needs to call a parent. Billy Underhill springs up; first, there is a joint to be smoked.

I've come out on to the balcony, careful not to wake the dogs. I want to put my face to the wind, but there is no wind, there is no cold. There is only heavy heat, stillness, even though I can see the minute movements of night shift workers toiling away in the hotel. Of all the things that betray you, the cold never does. It's clean and fierce, and it will kill you. Heat is not clean, and its method of killing you is to wear you down. Heat makes you stupid. Look at me here, standing in the desert, my face pointed north, trying to feel the cold of my past.

I can hear the blizzard winds howling down the school hallway as I open my locker to a small avalanche of papers, make-up, pens, textbooks. Before I can bend down and start to pick anything up, Leslie is there on her knees, gathering everything together as her friend Mary waits.

"Don't."

She stands, holding half my stuff.

"We're going to make a German Chocolate cake," she says.

Her last words, to me, at least. I don't know what German Chocolate cake is, so the last word she hears from me is, "Oh." Six years later, I will be walking along 2nd Avenue near 28th street in Manhattan when I happen to look into a bakery and see a German Chocolate cake in the window. Waiting behind a long queue of stout women in fur coats, I finally get to ask the woman behind the counter what is in the cake. When she says that it contains, among its many ingredients, coconut, I realize that's what I had seen in Mary's hand while Leslie was down on the floor picking up my stuff.

Leslie and Mary head down the hall, passing the classroom where Lena, always one to finish things up, is staying behind to polish off the final few rows to a dickie she is knitting for Leslie, who runs hot, so never likes to wear the whole sweater. It was supposed to be for the family ski trip, but that is off now and my father's fault. I know Lena couldn't care less, nor Leslie. But Heather, Liv tells us later at the hospital, when she is still missing, and everyone fears she too has been attacked was furious.

"She had a fit."

For me, there is only Billy and the killer joint. I find him hovering by the radiator in the back vestibule of school with a couple of our friends smoking as he calls them, "His warm-up joints." Other kids stream past us, ignoring the reek, as they dash out to waiting cars, one, I realize, is Liv's. She has come to pick up the girls. I should tell her that Leslie has gone to Mary's and that I haven't seen Lena or Heather, but Billy's hash is strong and my limbs heavy. But when the emptiness makes her idling ridiculous, I press myself up against the radiator to gather in as much heat as I can before I close my coat and run out.

Liv reaches over and opens the passenger side door, and I slip in as the CBC announcer intones,"Storm of the Century."

"They are predicting that there will be well over 120 centimetres," she says. "I was sitting here trying to work out in my head how many inches that is. Do you know?"

I don't. Of course, I don't.

"Well, that's one thing we can't blame on the Separatists. Only America will be left muddling along in feet and inches."

Liv stares off into the middle distance for a moment. "Let's see…215…I think that's over seven feet! Good Heavens!"

We both look at the bone-bleached frozen ground rapidly disappearing under the accumulating razor flakes.

"I'm glad I put my snakes out," Liv says. "The wind just whistles through the apartment."

We had snakes made by Lena. The windows at 456 were drafty, but Mother never used them. She would have thrown them out, hating the googly eyes and the sliver of a tongue sewn on the bean-filled tubes, but I stopped her.

The school door opens. We lean forward to see who it is, but it is only Billy taking an imaginary toke of a joint.

"Are you waiting for the girls?"

"Not waiting. Hoping. I was hoping I could corral one of them into coming with me as I drop off the turkeys. It's the least we can do, give a turkey to some poor family..."

"I think Leslie went to her friend Mary's."

"Oh," Liv sighs. "Terrible to think someone has already died."

"Is that why you're bringing a turkey?"

"No, no. On the radio. They reported it on the news. A man didn't want his Christmas Santa to get blown from the roof. He ended up getting blown off instead. An hour from now, he probably wouldn't have died. He would have just fallen into a snowdrift."

"What an idiot."

"Don't say that. Don't say that about something so sad."

I have never been alone with Liv before. I need to get out of the car.

Liv notices, and nods.

"You don't want to get trapped in here with me, snowed in, or snowed under, whatever the expression is. But if you do see any of my girls, tell them I put out cups for hot chocolate."

"You did?"

Liv smiles, "I don't normally. I hate the thought of objects, like cups, set up, waiting in an empty house. But, I guess some storm mentality kicked in. On the way over here, I popped into the store and bought three gallons of milk! Piers will think I'm mad. But I couldn't help myself."

Again, I reach for the door.

"Wait! Mab!"

Mother, her voice brassy and rich, comes through the fine stereo, promising to reveal a thing or two about her real feelings about Canadian winter storms.

"Should be fun."

I shrug and open the door only to have a gust of fierce wind, grab it, and pull me halfway out. I walk gingerly around the front of the car, half in dumb show, as if crossing a skating rink, but Liv, listening to the radio, isn't watching me. Back inside, the heavy reek of hashish, radiator heat, and bad breath fills the vestibule.

I see now that there is a man below on the street waiting at the bus stop. It's three o'clock in the morning; there won't be a bus for hours. Who is he? A soul forgotten by one of the night buses bringing the workers home? But the men are all lined up and counted off each night. Perhaps he slipped away, wanted to walk along the beach and hear the Gulf's lapping waves, anything other than the racket of construction. He is utterly still. You see lone men in the strangest of places, walking along a stretch of highway with no exit in sight, or way out in the desert, a mere dot, but moving at a pace steady enough to catch your eye. I was in Africa once working on a film. We had been driving through the flat Kenyan tundra for hours, nothing impeding our progress except the slight wobble you feel when staring too long at shimmering heat. Then, far off in the distance, an ancient Turkana appeared walking with a staff. Had we stopped and asked if he were lost, he would have thought us mad. The man down below, unaware that he's being spied on, does he feel any sense of dislocation? Or is here, now, enough?

Liv is gone when Billy and I and a couple of other friends abandon the vestibule and go running out into the storm. First, the wind is with us, then against us. Breathless, we duck down between two parked cars, snowdrifts at either end, and Billy pulls out the big joint. Six lighters, set on high, torch it into life. Deep drags are needed to keep it from sputtering out. The smoke sears my lungs, so I lift my head above the car hood, drink in the snow on the air. Billy stands and unzips his pants

"Pissing in the wind!"

Again we are running. Someone falls and makes a face-down snow angel. Coldness starts to seep through. The storm has turned. Has grown too strong for us. We huddle close, each tethered to the next so we won't lose each other. Billy, in the lead, pulls us towards the Coffee House. C is fascinated with the Coffee House, finds it unbelievable that an entire Victorian house would be given over to high school kids so they would have a place to hang out. There was a health clinic upstairs where those far cooler than me would get their clap jabs. It was run by a woman name Marjorie something, and it was said that she was the Maggie in Rod Stewart's "Maggie May." I would stare at this haggard woman; her neck weighed down by chunky Native Canadian jewellery, her short fingers gnarled by arthritis and topped with black nail polish and think Rod Stewart fucked that? Marjorie took a liking to me, which I interpreted to mean that I had the makings of a groupie.

We tumble through the door and, by habit, stand stamping our feet while knocking snow off our shoulders. The rush of warmth makes me feel very stoned. The rooms, while large, and the windows tall, feel like a bunker, subterranean and airless.

Alone, I go into the former front parlour and sit with my back against the wall needing to feel grounded. Then I hear Mother's voice. Not rich and brassy like it sounded in Liv's car, but a shitty, tinny whine coming from a blown speaker wedged high up in the corner. The storm could have been the only reason the radio was tuned to C.B.C. instead of CHOM FM, a station that was equally addicted to playing "Stairway to Heaven" as it was to the constant loop of "Tubular Bells."

Damn. There are no batteries in this Walkman. I thought it felt a bit light. There might be some here at the bottom of C's bag. Yes.

I know every word on this tape and yet to hear Mother's voice, young, strong, is giving me pause. I remember visiting her at the radio studio, the soundproof room, the microphones suspended in mid-air, raised or lowered depending on the height of the reader. That day the producer had wanted her to write something funny about the storm. But she never liked the extremes of Montreal weather. I once found her in tears because spring had come on with promiscuous abandon, and a plant had grown up overnight and into the car engine.

All of Montreal is tuned to C.B.C radio, listening to

my Mother. My Father is as he gathers up his papers to meet Piers. Leslie and Mary, who will have to abandon their cake when Mary's mother arrives home earlier than expected, are tuned in. Liv, not sure whether she should press on and deliver the last of the turkeys to the O'Connell family, still has the radio on. I'm hanging onto Mother's words as I try to un-stone myself, try not to look out the window at the storm and its horizontal mayhem. Lena, back at her home, the dickie done, is listening too.

Heather?

Lena told me once that she snapped off the radio even at the promos for Mother. But where is she? Timelines were drawn up, but her exact whereabouts have never been firmly established. If she was at home, then she had left again. If she was still at school, no one saw her. Not until Billy spots her, a spectral figure in the snow. But I'm getting ahead of myself.

And Frances? Frances. I know now where she was, alone in the basement playroom waiting for the principal, who was himself most anxious to get home, while he tries to phone our house hoping someone will pick up. He knew mother wasn't there. His radio is on, and he knows well enough trying to get through to anyone at C.B.C. during a storm is next to impossible.

The necessary clothing required for these Canadian winters: the snow pants, the coats, the boots, the scarves, the mittens are bad enough, but it's the attitude of my children that nearly breaks me. "Can't you even try?" I wail as I struggle with one flaccid foot, or hand, after the other. My ex-husband, on the other hand, revels in winter. For as long as I can remember, he has been waiting for the next ice age. A practical man, he felt when the children were young that they should get a jump on their survival skills. Miles and my girls must have spent countless hours planning for the ice apocalypse. How to drive a dog sled, build an igloo, and sup on whale blubber under a midnight sun.

My first winter here required every survival skill I had. In escaping post-war Britain, I left behind, I thought, everything dreary, and old, and worn out only to find dullness replaced by fear. Everything terrified me: the high skies, the wild ice floes rearing up in the St. Lawrence River, the ice-slicked streets, the wind through barren trees. But I think I was most frightened by the thought that all this was happening with me clinging to the edge of a vast empty continent. The only way I survived this wildness was by turning my fear into humour. But now, with the storm of the century raging outside, I find humour has failed me. I don't find it funny. I hate it. I'm scared. I think the weather is an ominous, malevolent force in all its incarnations. Sometimes I feel like I'm the only one who understands how terrible it is to be caught up in this universal condition called weather. It is unceasing, inescapable, and from one day to the next, all of us have to live through it with no control whatsoever over what rains down on us.

How prophetic Mother was.

On how many different tape recorders over the years have I played this? One day it might be too much of a relic, and I won't be able to find a cassette player, or I'll lose the tape. Maybe cassettes will make a comeback like vinyl has. My Mother's professional voice is much more British than her normal voice. If it's the last thing to survive of her, then it is yet another thing that doesn't speak the truth.

I think of me, standing at the window, aware of being close to Billy, the two of us leaning forward slightly to watch a girl, who, after a moment, we realize is Leslie, moving through the snow. She looks as elemental as the storm, and with that, strangely patient letting the mad currents of air twist her this way and that. When she disappears from view, Billy turns to me and says, "You gotta buy me a burger."

What if? From now on, the "what if"s comes into play. I hate "what if." But when the "this is" makes no real sense, not now, and not then, what are you left with except "what if?"

What if my father hadn't gone to meet Piers? He would not have gotten drunk, and being drunk saved Lena's life. If he hadn't gone to meet Piers, Frances and I wouldn't have met Heddou Marco, who, with his unwitting calmness and grace helped Frances and me find a reprieve from what we assumed would be the only horror that day.

But my Father did meet Piers. And, as he would tell Mother and me during that long night we spent huddled in my parents' former marriage bed, slowly drinking whiskey, when he first entered the Peel Street Pub he was taken aback.

"It reminded me of the war—same hysterical bonhomie. Every time the door opened and another person was blown in, a cheer went up, and shots went down. I had about five whiskeys before Piers showed up, looking his usual dour self. He merely nodded when he heard the cheer and then took me by the arm and said, "Let's go in the back, away from this bloody rabble."

I felt Mother move beside me. She was about to point out that they had once been best friends and business partners, but she checked herself. The things said that night could bear no mark of rancour.

Why did Piers hate my father so much? Was it because only after he and Liv had wed that they found out that her complicated birth with Lena had left her infertile? Was it that there was a child, not his, to remind him that he would never have a natural-born offspring? When Piers found out that Mab was pregnant with Frances, Lena told me, he said it was repulsive that a woman over forty should find herself entangled in something so guttural as childbirth. I wouldn't be surprised if my father felt the same way.

At the back of the pub, Piers plies my father with a few more drinks before letting him know that he has no intention of buying the inventory of high-end cars, claiming most were nothing but heaps of junk.

I remember us still on the bed and my father reaching over and taking the whiskey bottle quite roughly out of Mab's hand. "The man wouldn't know a sound car from a Tonka Truck."

What would my father have made of this city, Abu Dhabi, a toy town in every way, zipped through by an endless parade of high-end cars? They are not the sort he loved, of course, not the beauties, the Austin-Healeys, the Bugattis (Oh, how excited he was when he stumbled upon a Bugatti Veyron) found in garages under tarps and then relieved of the mouse nests and misguided tires, the cracked seats and the streaks of rust and slowly brought back to life. I miss him. Each time some wealthy pup blasts by in his Ferrari or Maserati, I feel a twinge of snobbishness. It kills me to think that Lena doesn't know he's dead. Or perhaps she does. I paid for his obituary to be carried in all the major Canadian papers.

My father poured himself a healthy shot and sat drinking silently. Mother sighed. I don't think she knew Daddy was planning on selling his company to Piers. They had been separated nearly a year, and yet I felt at times throughout the night her arm, supposedly around my shoulder to comfort me, reaching, trying to touch my father.

"At least you were having a booze up. While you were with Piers, I was desperately trying to think of something else to say about the storm. My producer wanted three more minute-forty-five spots."

"Oh, yes. Did you come up with anything?"

"No, not really." Mum leaned down and picked up her purse, a floppy bag that made it hard for me to quickly find her change purse and steal ten or twenty bucks. She rooted around a minute, then pulled out a crumpled up piece of paper and started to read.

Weather story #1

On my brother's eighth birthday, it rained all morning. My mother was in a temper. She hadn't gotten the laundry in on time. But it wasn't just a matter of wet clothes. It was that they were wet and covered in coal. London was in the middle of a fog crisis. Nobody used the word "pea-souper." But that didn't change the fact that just breathing left an oily slick in your mouth.

Sam had been given new shoes for his birthday. There is a famous picture of an East End boy excitedly grasping his new shoes, his old ones still on, frayed, scuffed, and untied. Not my brother. Sam put on his shoes right away and then went down to the Thames. Nobody heard him slide into the water or cry out. My mother never knew who or what to blame: the shoes for being slippery, herself for buying them, or Sam for being so stupid.

Weather Story #2

I fell in love and was naïve enough to believe that what my husband liked I would like. Then I was naïve enough to believe we could like different things. Then I had a baby. I wasn't crazy about the name Augusta, but my husband thought it might smooth some ruffled feathers, his mother's in particular. I came up with the nickname Augati, which most people pronounce incorrectly and which, when she was young, my daughter hated because the Romper Room woman never, ever saw her through that ridiculous magic looking-glass.

Right after Augati was born, I assumed my husband, who loved to fly having been an RAF pilot after the war, would stay on the ground. He thought differently. Augati was born on a Tuesday. On Saturday, Miles went flying; I got a call from the airport telling me that all radio contact had been lost. I looked out the window. The sun was shining.

"But, it's so lovely out."

"Oh, don't go by what you see on the ground," I was told. "There are terrible high-level disturbances."

Since then, I have never been able to trust what I see out the window. Is that sunny day real?

Weather story #3

The Blitz and bad storms are very similar, same boredom, the same dull absence of choice. Some people are excited by such over-the-top displays, people like my ex-husband, for instance. Of course, he got to count the shiny Luftwaffe as they flew over his house in Kent on their way to try and annihilate London, the East End docks in particular, where I was, huddled down in the basement of my family's trembling house, breathing in the sour smell of my parents and their fear..."

"I take it none of this made it to air?" my Father said, dryly.

Mother laughed softly. "No."

My parents were doing what everyone feels the need to do on the far side of a catastrophe; you place yourself in time and space. "I was..." "I remember it so clearly, we were..."

They didn't notice that I was staying silent. I only joined the conversation when our recounting of the day reached the point when Frances was safely home, and Heddou was with us. To speak of anything before that would have been too shameful. I was still coming to grips with the fact that that day's horrors could have been so much worse and all my fault.

Billy and I, now starving, the munchies descending as it does, are foolishly throwing on our coats and barely bothering with our hats, gloves, and scarves. Costa's cafe is just across the road with its promise of a burger and some fries. The storm takes us headlong and delivers us half-frozen, ears burning, noses running, fingers stiff.

Costa cries out, "Closed," but when he sees us in such a sorry state, he waves us in and throws two flat, grey patties on the grill.

We sit in the window booth. A few cars are crawling along, and we see one slide through the intersection and nearly hit someone. Billy says, "It's Heather." She enters at the moment that might have been her exit. But the car misses her, and she heads home.

Nothing gnaws at my brain; nothing sparks. Instead, Billy tells me that Heather had once said he ate like a bovine and that it wasn't until nearly a year later, he realized what bovine meant. He laughs, his mouth full of burger and fries. I eat my hamburger with the pronounced concentration of the very stoned. Costa comes over to hurry us along. He will never get home if he doesn't close up now. He tells us we are crazy not to have heeded the school warnings. Billy rolls his eyes. Authority, benevolent or not, is not to be taken seriously. His father, Mick Underhill, a dyspeptic Irish drunk, a man so thin that I wondered if when naked, you could see his organs; a fine, shadowy gas works, churning away, had long lost the power to inflict any damage on Billy or his older brother Seamus. I love Billy for taking this newfound freedom and turning it into a sweet-toned "Fuck you" to anyone who tries to tell him what to do.

We spend a long time bundling up, tucking in, and making sure there are no gaps. The minute we step outside, our efforts are blown to shit.

"Ten steps forward. Ten steps back." I yell.

Above Billy's scarf, I can see his brow knit. "Wouldn't that bring you back to where you began?"

"No! Ten steps FACING forward. Ten-steps FACING backward."

Billy raises his hand. We aren't going in the same direction.

It takes me forever to get home. I keep having to shelter in doorways to catch my breath. The snow is already nearly impossible to walk through, and I repeatedly fall. I pass Frances' school. Nothing occurs to me, or if it did, I assume she would have gone home hours ago.

Again, this mental game, this ongoing calculation of where all of us were at various points during the day. Liv will have realized, about the time I am walking home, that she will get stuck at the O'Connell's if she doesn't impose and ask at least some of the O'Connell boys if they would be so kind and help shovel out her car. My father is waiting for Piers to arrive, and both Lena and Leslie are home. The skis are still lined up, which the girls find strange. Heather had thrown such a fit when Piers told them the ski trip was off. Not that they could have departed that day, not with this storm.

As I am making my way along Sherbrooke Street, Frances decides she doesn't want to stay at school any longer. The principal isn't that nice a man that she wants to spend a whole night with him. Besides, the chocolate milk from a carton he gave her just before he went upstairs yet again to see if he can contact anyone to pick her up, has made her feel sick. She slips out of the basement and up to her classroom where the cloakroom door is open; hers the only snowsuit left. It is a fiddly business getting it on. I had pinched her hard only that morning because she kept squirming while I was trying to hook the straps on her snow pants. These, however, she manages, it is the jacket zipper that she can't get now. And, her scarf, which she hates anyway, not liking the feeling of frozen drool, isn't going around her head in the same way I had tied it. As for her rubber boots, they never snapped easily.

I turn up Victoria Avenue, barely making headway, as Frances steps from school and starts across the playing field. I see her, with her determined four-square walk, ploughing ahead until the sheer physical weight of the snow begins to overwhelm her. As I finally reach our steps, a veritable mountainside, so much so that twice I slide half-way back down, Frances is crying out, but there was no-one, even if there were, the wind makes a mockery of her cries for help. And, as I fell through the front door and lay winded and defrosting, a police car, its chains as muffled as slippers on a carpet, slows when the cop spots some movement. Intuition alone had him bounding across the field to pull her out, this half-frozen child.

Here, on this hot balcony, there is no forgiveness, no excuse. Frances nearly froze to death, and it was my fault. I am still on the floor when she is brought upstairs, thawed enough for a barrage of muted, weak punches to fall all about me as she cries, "You forgot me! You forgot me!" I want her to hit me forever. She soon tires, but as I try to get up to thank the policeman, Frances refuses to let me move, and he leaves without me getting his name. Still, he's here in my mind, a saviour, standing above us, his boots leaving puddles of melt on the carpeting.

It's weird how a quiet this deep presses in on your ears as if the absence of sounds leaves more room for gravity or perhaps a rise or drop in barometric pressure. Montreal, that night, Christmas Eve, was utterly silent as well. Most of the roads had yet to be cleared, and the houses themselves were held fast, often above the first-story windows, by the snowdrifts. Even so, Christmas would dawn, and, like Frances sleeping down the hall, little kids, ignoring the particular disquiet of their parents, would agitate to be allowed to open their presents. Mother had managed, before we had congregated on the bed, to remember to hang Frances' stocking.

I wonder if my parents were aware of the unnerving silence? Does mother now, when the palm trees with their firework fronds outside France's window cease to clatter, does she think about that night as the three of us lay on her bed, none of us knowing if Lena would survive or not?

Eventually, what with Frances' soaked-through snowsuit and my soaked-through coat, hat, and scarf, we begin to feel itchy, hot, and uncomfortably wet, and she climbs off me. I help her peel off her clothes, and we put our boots up on the radiator. Together we go into her room, and I find a pair of pajamas for her to put on even though it was still early afternoon. Together we go to my room, and I too put on my pajamas, and I say we should plug in the Christmas tree lights. I don't think until I go to the window to see what the storm is doing, that we are more than a few inches apart. I turn on the TV, an American station out of Plattsburg comes in the clearest. The weatherman, normally relegated to late in the program, is sitting at the anchor desk. The storm is actually three storms, he tells us, one churning up the east coast, another swooping down from Canada, and a third, a lake effect storm off the Great Lakes which is being sucked in and gathering strength from the other two. The female anchor shakes her head. All so hard to fathom, she seems to say. Then she turns to the camera and advises everyone to stay indoors, even Rufus, she smiled.

"Who's Rufus?" Frances asks.

"I think she means that even our dogs and cats should stay indoors."

I get up and look out the window. Can you see three storms meeting? Is that why the winds seem to howl in one direction before completely reversing themselves? Instead, I see a car sliding down the hill backward.

My father nodded when I told him that I happened to be at the window.

"I couldn't," he said, "stand Piers' company one second longer. I should have thrown a drink in his face, something. Instead, I threw twenty dollars down on the table and walked out. I headed off blindly when I noticed this cab, well the bugger didn't know what the hell he was doing. He hailed me. Before I even reached him, the driver was rappelling himself around the front of the car, leaving me to drive."

"Heddou," I said.

"Was that his name?"

"Yes."

"He had never seen snow before. The poor bastards brought up here, promised the bloody earth, all for their vote, and then what? Half of them are freezing to death. I tried to show him a thing or two. Told him that one mustn't hit the brakes hard when you start to skid, but he just stared fixedly ahead. Didn't seem to hear a thing."

"Why were you coming down the hill backward?" I asked.

Frances doesn't believe me when I tell her to come quickly that there is a car out of control. She pushes herself in front of me, and I wipe clear the lower part of the window so she can see for herself.

"I wasn't out of control," My father frowned, "Far from it. With a front-engine, I figured the weight of the car would have us facing forward by the time we reached Chesterfield."

He must have figured wrong because when the car did swing around frontwards, it bangs right into a tree.

It stays there, the snow piling up in the windscreen until...

Frances and I think it is a dog.

Whatever it is, we see it the same moment as the as yet unknown occupants of the cab do.

It is Frances who says, "That's Daddy."

I see him then too, see him crawling his way over the drifts to the dog, see him followed by a black man who has on only the thinnest jacket. Together they pick up the; I nearly push my head through the window, trying to see what it is.

A person? Yes, a person or a dog? I can't tell. It has to be a person because my father has lain it in the back seat with great care. Then he starts shouting something at Heddou while pointing up to our flat before leaping back in the car. The force, the sheer will of man and machine to move seamlessly through the solid mass of opaque whiteness. He is gone, swallowed by the storm in an instant. Frances and I, as if on cue, go to the front door and wait.

The man down below at the bus stop has just walked out into the middle of the road. He's standing there. He'll see me if he looks up, or maybe not. I haven't turned on the balcony light. It's hard to imagine that the day will dawn, a bus will come, and he will be absorbed by the work-a-day world. He is singular now, a man apart, and a mystery. He seems to like being in the middle of the road. This is a city of workers, and yet I don't see much evidence of them. Sometimes, in a brightly lit cafe, I'll spot them playing dominos, smoking, and drinking tea, but should all the workers disappear overnight, the city would stand empty, yes, but unchanged.

When the Haitians started arriving in Montreal in the early '70s, I remember seeing houses, brown, winter-worn, being given the once over, the crude yet desperate spray of blues and pinks, intoxicating but deeply out of place. The French-speaking Haitians with their garish houses, we Anglos believed, had been lured up by the Separatist government to pad the votes. Whatever the case, my father was right; they were woefully unprepared for their first few winters. Heddou had only been in Montreal three months when that storm hit, a storm which still hasn't been matched in terms of the amount of snow dumped on the city or in the fierceness of the winds. Twenty or more people died because of it. Their deaths would have been the story of the day, if not for my family.

It takes Heddou a long time to arrive at our door. I suppose he isn't sure he is going up the right steps, but when he sees us standing, staring down at him, he bows slightly, then takes off his Florsheim shoes. Frances, very solemnly, picks them up, and, after moving aside her drying boots, lays them out on the radiator. I can see that the leather is already cracked. In his stocking feet, Heddou slumps down on the top step, where he remains for a long time. Frances and I don't know what to do, but we aren't frightened. I can't help noticing that the snow sits lightly on his head, and when it does melt, his hair glistens.

"Did our father send you with a message?"

Heddou looks up. Tears stream down his face. "Cette fille dans la neige."

I ask if he speaks English. Frances pinches me. She is right; it is rude to ask.

Heddou buries his head back into his arms and begins to cry. I don't think Frances has ever seen a man cry before. So much is hidden, especially from a child. She backs away and knocks one of his shoes off the radiator.

"Sir?" I reach out and touch his shoulder. "Would you like to come inside and sit down? The house it's getting cold."

Heddou looks up, and I motion toward the living room. Instead, he comes in and sits on a small wicker chair in the hallway. It creaks beneath him. The chair is not meant for sitting on. Not in this century, anyway. I close the door. The radiators, always noisy, start to clang and knock. Frances nudges me.

"You should make him tea."

Not wanting Heddou to think we are abandoning him, we slowly back into the kitchen. I can see that he is now surreptitiously grinding his thawing feet into the carpet, trying to relieve a prickly itch he has probably never felt before in his life.

Once the kettle has boiled, I place on a small tray two Peek Freans Shortbread cookies and a cup of tea. One sip, and he grimaces.

"Sucre?"

"What?"

"Sucre?"

"Sugar? Oh sorry. I didn't think." I reach for his cup. "How many?"

He holds up five fingers. "Cinq."

"Five? Wow."

"Is that allowed?" Frances asks.

"I guess."

Back in the kitchen, Frances counts as I hack at the hardened brown sugar.

"The most Mummy ever allows is three."

"He's a grown-up. He can have as many as he likes."

"Oh," she says, then pauses. "Who was that girl?"

"You think it was a girl?"

"Yeah."

"I don't know."

"Sally, the deaf girl?"

"Why her?"

"Because she couldn't cry out for help."

"She can make noise. Just not words."

"But how would she know she was making noise in all that wind if she can't hear herself?"

I don't think it is Sally. Wrong ankles, wrong weight. The girl, or woman, is thin.

"And, why was she bleeding?" Frances leans over to breathe in the deep sweetness of the tea.

"She was bleeding?"

143

"The snow was red."

"I didn't see that."

"I did. I saw it."

I pick up the tea and bring it back to Heddou. He takes a sip then starts to cry again, turning his head, desperate to hide his tears.

"Monsieur, la fille?" I ask. "Où est la fille?"

Heddou says something, shaking his head, but his words are low, creamy almost, and nonsensical. He tries again, but adding more words only makes it worse. Marooned in our separate languages, Heddou begins to murmur, then to sway, his eyes rolling back and forth. This must be praying, I think.

Now, I am not so sure. Some things are just too fucking unbelievable. I can imagine the litany marauding through Heddou's mind: the folly of his hopes; the city all around him, hunched in on itself, given over to darkness by three in the afternoon; the bare trees and the missing birdsong; the cold, the ever-present cold that wiped out the sun's heat and pale rays; the unholy storm that obliterated all before him; and now, a girl in the snow, near death. No wonder his eyes were rolling around in his head.

"I want beans on toast," Frances says.

I haven't thought about food. I have been staring stupidly at the TV screen while never forgetting for a moment that there is a black man whose Florsheim shoes are cracking to bits on the radiator sitting on a wicker chair that might very well collapse beneath him. The phone hasn't rung. Later we would learn the lines were down in parts of the city but not the same parts where the electricity had gone out. But the minute Frances says she wanted beans on toast, I realize that I too am starving.

"Ok, I'll make us some."

"Will you make some for that man?

"I guess. I mean, shouldn't I?"

Frances twists her mouth. "Make two tins," then calls after me as I head to the kitchen, "And make sure you get the butter in all the corners."

Out in the hallway, Heddou sits. At least, he isn't grinding his feet into the carpet anymore. He looks hollowed out, a defeated man.

"Manger?" I ask.

"Non, non, non." He doesn't want to be an imposition.

"Oui? Beans avec toast. Pour moi et moi petite soeur. Et vous?"

"Non, non."

I should just bring him some. In the kitchen, I open three tins of Libby's baked beans and from each one fish out the chunk of fat before dumping it in the pot. I cut the bread into thick slices. If it is possible, the storm seems to have intensified. The door to the back balcony is repeatedly being sucked in then pushed out by the battering winds, and the street beyond obliterated. I try to ignore it and keep quiet any thoughts of suffocation.

I bring Heddou his plate. He stands, and I see him hesitate. The beans, I suppose, are a shock, brown, and sweet instead of black and savoury. The bread too. But I knew nothing of Caribbean cooking then.

Frances pushes her toast loaded with beans to the very edge of the plate and starts to nibble. It is all part of a burgeoning rebellion against my Father's sublime table manners and his demand that we chew thirty-two times.

When I think Heddou has finished, I go to collect his plate. He reaches for his wallet, and for one horrifying moment, I think he is going to try and pay me. Instead, he pulls out a photo and hands it to me. I have to put the plates down on the floor to take it. It is a picture of a pale blue cottage, far paler than the violent hues that have been painted on the houses in Montreal. But maybe the tropical sun made subtle what our short summers never could. It looks, too, like it must be on a beach or near one.

"Belle," I say.

"Can I see it?" Frances pulls my hand down. "Is it a real house?"

"Yeah."

Frances traces the outline of the cottage before handing it back to Heddou. I pick up the plates, go into the kitchen to wash them. When I come out again, I can see that the bottom drawer of the old chest-of-drawers in the living room is open. Solemnly, Frances is ferreting through all the family photos, pulling one picture out at a time, and then bringing it to Heddou, where she explains who is who and where they are before returning it and coming back with another.

"That's my dad's car," she says, showing him a picture of my father in a classic Jag. "Well, not his car. But one of many that he gets to use. We're not millionaires or anything. I never get to sit in the front seat in case I kick the gears or get my grimy fingers all over everything."

Heddou opens his eyes wide to show how impressed he is. Frances hands him another. It is my Father and Lena.

"Mon Pere...la fille de mon Pere...Lena. Autre Maman," I say, though why I need to say she was from another mother, I have no idea.

I see now Heddou looking hard at the picture. I should have known then, especially when he seems reluctant to hand it back. But the moment passes when he formally introduces himself. We all shake hands. Frances goes to get another picture and I say, "I think he's seen enough."

We watch "The Man from Uncle." We watch "The Avengers." Frances falls asleep, and I must have drifted off for a bit because when I come to the news is on. The storm has lost none of its power; even fury can become monotonous. I notice the sound of buzzing engines. I go to the window where below I can see snowmobiles crisscrossing the street, revving up and down snowbanks impervious to the fact that buried beneath them might be a car, or a prized bush, or a mailbox.

The doorbell rings. Heddou is tucking in his shirt and casting about for his shoes.

"Police," he whispers. I must look terrified because he lays a reassuring hand on my shoulder and says, "Ouvrez la porte."

Two policemen, dusted with snow, come up the stairs, but they ignore me and start talking to Heddou, who stands nodding.

"J'ai pense," he says, quietly.

Heddou sits back down on the rickety chair. His shoes, dried jerky, are difficult to slip into. The policemen and I watch until he finally stands, grimacing in pain.

"We will take your leave, Mademoiselle."

"Why?"

"Your mother is due presently."

"Can't he stay?"

"That would be impossible."

Heddou gives me a quick squeeze.

"A Bientot."

I lean in, hugging him, fearing to let go. As soon as they are down the stairs, I go back to the window. Below idles a Snow Cat. I see Heddou give a nervous laugh before being helped up. As it ploughs away, another Snow Cat comes down the hill and stops on the same spot. The door opens. Mother falls forward out of the cab, sinking into the snow up to her armpits. Two policemen rush to help her.

Mother should be in a temper; she should feel humiliated and raging against the preposterousness of snow mounted up like mountains. She should be telling me to stop looking the idiot as she does whenever I seem anxious. Instead, she says, "I need to get out of these clothes before anything." I follow her, watch as she takes off her work clothes and puts on an old pair of Indian drawstring pants.

"Has your Father called?"

"No."

"The phones must still be out."

That hadn't occurred to me; we had T.V. after all. I reach and pick up the receiver on the phone by the bed. Nothing. Not even static.

"I need a drink."

Again, I follow, watching as she takes a bottle of vodka from the fridge and pours herself a large shot and then another. Neither of us notices that Frances has woken and now stands sleepily in the doorway.

"They don't know..." Mother says her back turned, cold glass burning her fingers, "...if she will live."

"Who?"

"Lena, darling. That was Lena in the snow."

As Mother collapses into the chair, her body heaving the first of many sobs, I feel Frances' sharp little fingers dig into my back.

Here.

Now.

In the desert with a man standing in the middle of the street.

I could be wrong; I could have imagined it all wrong. The police forensics might have gotten it wrong too. I read In Cold Blood. Footprints criss-cross. One mortally wounded victim moves. One mortally wounded victim stays where they were struck. Murderers panic. Blood is alive. Blood moves. Is moved. Stops in its tracks. Frances has made herself something of an expert on murder. She spends half her free time watching these bizarre TV shows in which sordid crimes are reenacted. Nothing is ever fully known, she tells me. Nothing is for sure.

But on the afternoon of December 23rd, Heather Driscoll sits in the living room, the tinsel on the Christmas tree stirring slightly, and listens as her two sisters chat in the kitchen. By the door are five sets of skis, boots, and poles. Her mother should have taken them downstairs to the storage locker. Something makes her get up, open the front door, walk down the three flights of stairs to the basement. It isn't a cold, musty place. The lockers and the hallway are well lit. The tenants in the high-end building use them to store everything from unused but perfectly good furniture to bikes and sporting equipment. Often when Liv is down there fetching her stepladder or storing large plastic containers full of winter coats or summer clothes, she will run into a neighbour doing the same thing. Heather, however, doesn't run into anyone. Though not an hour before Mrs. Taylor, who lives opposite, had sent her husband down to see if he could root out another space heater even though he told her it was all in her head that she felt a chill. "Head or not, I'm cold."

Heather finds the ax where it always is, leaning up against the wall behind the woodpile. Piers insists on keeping one even though the wood delivered for the fireplace was cut to size, nicely tempered, and stacked with geodesic precision.

There is some evidence that Heather swung the ax a few times, lodging it in one of the two by four cross beams of the locker. Practice? Or was that when the compulsion, the need was born?

With all the snowmelt from Lena and Leslie's boots, not to mention her own, her stocking feet are soaked. This either gives her extra traction or saves Lena's life. In any case, there is no hesitation; Heather walks into the kitchen where Leslie is stirring chocolate on the stove. She raises the ax and brings it down, splitting Leslie's head open. The sound is terrible, though Leslie does not scream or, at least, no neighbour hears any screams. The sound then must be from her skull cracking open. Brain material (I always wondered about those two words together, but I suppose they needed to differentiate between bone material or even metal fragments from the ax) is found in the chocolate and on the stove. Leslie, herself, is not found for many hours.

Lena, at the kitchen table, on one of the benches (Piers thought chairs with backs would thwart the desire to sit straight), leaps up raising her arm in an attempt to prevent Leslie from receiving another blow. Her right arm is nearly severed at the shoulder. That she isn't cracked over the head as she gets between Heather and Leslie might come down to Heather's wet stocking feet and the amount of blood on the floor. Heather slips, and Lena flees. Leslie is killed instantly. Maybe that is enough, or maybe Heather, like her sisters, hates to leave anything a mess. Whatever the reason, she doesn't pursue Lena, who manages to run through the snow, with her arm half off the ten blocks to our house. What would I have done had she showed up at the door gravely wounded? In the years to come, I wished that. I wanted to be the one who saved Lena, not the one who nearly killed Frances.

It turns out blood congeals very quickly when there isn't a beating heart sending it out at regular pulses. Heather rolls Leslie in an old rug and hides her behind the couch. Not a hiding place as such, but not where anyone will think to look. The blood in the kitchen is cleaned up with rags that Liv keeps under the kitchen sink. Heather must assume that Lena is dead and buried under the snow because she doesn't rush. She makes sure the place is wiped clean.

Liv, at the O'Connell's, is having yet another cup of tea. The boys have tried to shovel her car out, but as the youngest tells her, "By the time you get one side clean, the other is covered again." If you realize later that you are eating a Peek Frean's cookie and drinking a cup of Red Rose tea, trying not to notice how stained and chipped the cup is, as your child is being murdered, does the ordinary ever reassert itself? But you can't go through life not having cups of tea, can you?

Piers is feeling smug at the same moment Heather raises the ax. Yet another negotiation in which he has bested my father. Seventeen years earlier, in a pub, much like Peel Street, they had ironed out the exchange of Liv. My Father felt there was no reason they shouldn't all be friends, for Lena's sake, if nothing else. But Piers quickly put the kibosh on that idea. He couldn't stand Mab, never understood what my Father saw in her. As for the business they had been partners in? Miles should be damn grateful that Piers didn't blacklist him.

Now, once again, Miles hasn't gotten what he wanted. Neither has Piers, but he hasn't lost anything either. With Miles gone, he sits and enjoys his wine before leaving the pub, but when he sees how bad the storm has become, he crosses the street to wait for the tempest to blow itself out from his office couch which it eventually does, but by then he had been found by the police.

We are parochial in our thinking when it comes to weather. A storm moves on, out to sea, and we don't think of it anymore. "We're not at sea!" But lying on my parent's bed, I did think about the winds that had nearly killed Frances and had pulled and bullied Lena as she stumbled her way towards us. I thought of them now battering Nova Scotia, creating a storm surge that piled the ice in the inlets and bays up onto the shore the force of the collision so loud that people far inland felt uneasy, as if the very earth beneath them was nothing more than an ice floe.

"She didn't make a sound! That enraged me," my father said, his voice catching. "If only she would have moaned or cried out, then, then, I would have known that she was fighting to survive. And I needed to know what happened. It was not like she'd been run over. It was as if she'd walked into a propeller."

I felt Mother beside me, shifting in an attempt to contain her emotions. The whole night before, we had known nothing of what was happening at the hospital. The phones were still out. The night didn't pass for us so much as it evaporated. Mother sat smoking in the living room with Frances asleep on the couch while I retreated to my room and spent the night on the windowsill, my head pressed against the cold glass. But now, the picture of what Lena had suffered was being made clear, and I think we were both afraid of delayed hysterics.

"Once at the hospital, it felt like time did not exist." My father continued. "I couldn't tell if I was thinking the same thoughts over and over or was just coming up with them. I threw my gloves away, but my coat was far bloodier, only later I thought to throw it out. An orderly kept coming in and mopping the wet floor, so it never got dry. I could see that the whole hospital was on an emergency footing, gurneys lined the walls, calls for doctors went out ceaselessly over the intercom, but I knew that wasn't because of Lena. I was afraid that maybe they had forgotten her, that she lay alone in some room, forgotten as doctors and nurses hurried past to deal with the storm victims. But I didn't get up to ask. I felt that it would only make things worse."

Mother nodded; normally, my father's reticence drove her crazy. But now she said, "I wondered what happened to your coat."

I didn't notice he is in shirt sleeves when at midday the police bring him home. The kitchen is stupidly bright and sunny. It's always something of an insult after a big storm, the high, cloudless days. He sits, whiskey in hand, and tells us that Lena is in a medically induced coma in intensive care. She has a catastrophic wound inflicted, they suspect, by an ax that has nearly severed her arm. The reason she didn't bleed to death is due to the storm, the cold and the snow acting to cauterize the wound. We are all listening so intently that it is a shock when he starts to cry. "The blow had missed a major artery by millimeters," he says, holding his glass out for another whiskey and Frances, taking advantage of his open arms, crawls into his lap.

Before Mother can pour him another drink, the phone rings. With a shaking hand, she reaches for it then hands it to Miles. He listens, displeased. The police want to interview me down at the station. And, Billy Underhill. Leslie's friend Mary and her Mother have already been in and told them all that they knew. (Yes, Leslie came over to bake a German chocolate cake, Mary's mother says, needing to defend herself. But then I had arrived home unexpectedly. After five miserable years of being a divorcee, I have just become engaged to a man I have known for a month. Can anyone blame me for wanting to speak to my daughter alone? Had I known...)

My father finishes his drink, then pours another to bring into the bedroom with him while he changes. Mother, out of habit, follows him in and is unable to stop herself from saying it is a good thing that she hasn't thrown out all his clothes. The doorbell rings as he is rooting around for a tie.

Once outside and seeing the police car, I hope that my

father will be told to sit in front, so no one will suspect we are being arrested. But the officer holds open the back door and ushers us in. The whole ride, we don't speak, although when the car fishtails as it turns onto Sherbrooke Street, he puts a steadying hand on my knee.

Two detectives are waiting for us. I have never been in a police station. There is no way not to feel culpable for crimes imagined. I have a fleeting glimpse of Billy Underhill with his father. From the way he is walking, I can tell he has seen the inside of a police station many times if only to bail his father out of the drunk tank. We have all been called in so the police can create a timeline. Billy and I had seen Heather last, a shadowy figure nearly getting hit by a car spinning through the intersection.

With both Leslie and Heather missing, and the snow having covered up whatever tracks there might have been, the police have very little to go on. What is known is that Heather dated older men, some of whom were not of the "highest character." Our detective is Québécois, and had trouble with his H's. This is the type of detail I obsess on now.

Before the detective can ask me any questions, he's called out of the room. My father exhales. But again we are silent until the detective returns and says, he'd like to speak to my father alone.

I understand everything then. I don't know how. But the story is no longer something I have to catch up with, each turn a shock. Instead, it is all dull inevitability. I knew it was Heather. I knew that my father had been called out because they had found Leslie. Not they. Liv. Liv had found her daughter stuffed behind the couch, found her as Piers fumed about the incompetence of the police. "Isn't it obvious that Heather has been kidnapped, her beauty finally failing to protect her?" Liv, who had never shared her doubts about Heather with her husband, sits on the couch listening, hating him until seized by a feeling of utter dread, she stands up and pulls, with astonishing strength, the sofa away from the wall.

I knew too that Heather was somewhere out in the city. She would know by this time that Lena had lived. And, she was not used to failure.

When my father comes back in the room, he tells me to put my coat on; we are leaving. Again, we drive silently back through the city. A few roads are ploughed, but most are still encased in snow except for Victoria Avenue. Here the snow is matted down, churned up, pitched aside, blackened fading to grey.

Upstairs, mother and Frances are waiting at the door.

"It was Heather," I say. My father turns to me, not with surprise but with a look of interminable sadness.

Heather's whereabouts are still unknown, so she has to be considered a threat. In the end, it turns out she was close by, a mere two blocks away having broken into a house on Lansdowne Avenue where she is found, naked, wrapped in a fur coat, in a closet. Lena, now Lena, when she wanted to disappear, well, fuck, gone.

My father has been offered police protection, which he refuses, not wanting to draw even more attention to the house. Frances, always one to intuit danger, says we must lock all the doors and the windows despite the fact we are on the third floor. She even has my father barricade the back balcony door pointing out that the snowdrifts are so high one could nearly climb right up to our flat.

We all stand and watch as my father puts not only a chair up against the balcony door but also finds a couple of wood planks and nails them across. Do we feel safe? That question again. No. We don't feel safe

Eventually, the three of us, the bottle of Irish mostly gone, fall asleep only to wake a few hours later to see Frances at the end of the bed. It is Christmas morning. She wants to open her big presents having already gone through her Christmas stocking: glitter make-up, an array of pens, Barbie outfits, a book of kid jokes, a Clementine, two Peek Freans shortcake cookies, and five thin mints.

We sit in our dressing gowns while Frances tears open the wrapping paper. We all try to ignore Lena's presents stacked to one side. I used to be jealous of that pile, an orgy of gifts on top of all the other ones Lena had already received.

"Open yours too, Aug."

I bend down and pick one up. My head throbs and my mouth is dry. My first hangover and kind of like a first orgasm: I had no real understanding of what was happening, that is, until the next one. My parents know how not to suffer. They sip Bloody Mary's but never think to offer me one.

Presents over, Mother goes into the kitchen and starts frying up kippers.

God, I hate that smell and say as much to Frances, who is lying on the couch playing with her new Barbie.

"I like it," she says, sniffing the air. "Almost as much as gasoline."

"I hate that smell too."

I pick up one of her Barbie's, an old one, and watch as

Frances struggles to get tiny high heels onto pointed rigid feet.

"Who's at Lena's house now?" she asks.

"What do you mean?" I lay back, letting the Barbie whose hair is cropped and who has holes through her tits where Frances has stuck pins, rest atop my breast.

"Leslie. Is Leslie still there?"

"I don't know. I don't think so."

"I keep thinking about her eye."

"Her eye?"

"The funny one. It always looked like it saw something I couldn't."

"Like what?"

"I dunno."

It's not seeing anything now; I want to say. But maybe Frances' is right. Leslie's wandering eye saw far more than we gave her credit.

We eat our breakfast without much pleasure listening to the Queen's Christmas message. Then one by one, we drop away from each other. I don't know what happened to our Christmas dinner. I have no memory of a turkey or bread left out to get stale for the stuffing. Perhaps, while she was cooking the kippers, Mother had thrown it all out. I fall asleep only to be woken once again by Frances.

"We've got to go to the hospital. Dad says."

Christmas carols are playing over the loudspeakers, and there is not one but two Santas handing out candy canes to visitors as they arrive at the hospital. Hot air is being blasted just inside the doors to jump-start people through the stomach-turning, antiseptic pong that seeps out of every pore of the building. We move in single file past the Santas and head for the elevator, Frances whipping her string-connected mittens in wild circles. The elevator door opens, and we have to stand aside as a child in a hospital bed is wheeled out.

"What's wrong with that boy?" Frances asks.

"Shush," Mother tells her.

"What?"

"In hospitals…," My father says, resting his hand on the back of her neck, "…you are not allowed to ask questions."

"Why?"

He tightens his grip and jostles her head.

"No questions. None. No, whys. No, who's. Nothing."

"But…"

"Nothing."

"But 'but' isn't a question."

"Frances."

I want to fucking scream. There is no way around it. We all become actors when reality outstrips our mind's comprehension.

The elevator doors open, and another Santa is holding a basket filled with candy canes as well as small wrapped gifts. He smells like a Christmas tree. Someone must have sprayed him with a pine scent. His red cheeks and robust smile does nothing to dispel the terror we are all feeling.

Frances accepts a striped cane and a small gift but immediately hands them to me. A nurse wearing floppy reindeer antlers points the way to Lena's room. There is a glass window running along each room for the nurses to keep an eye on their patients so we can see Lena, see the breathing tubes down her throat, the thick bandage binding her chest, the machines humming and beeping.

We stop at the threshold of her door, having lost all courage to move forward.

It is Frances who breaks the spell and pushes past us. "Lena!" she cries as she starts to crawl up on the bed.

For some reason, I marked this arbitrary moment as the end, it's far from it. Liv arrives absentmindedly holding the token gift Santa has given her. There are the doctor updates, so many and with so little change that before the day is out, we all stop standing expectedly. There are the weeks visiting the hospital that bleed into boredom. The snowmelt surprises us, as does the new leaves. There is the day when we are told that the best place for Lena to undergo her rehabilitation would be in New Orleans among Vietnam vets who have also suffered catastrophic injuries. There is the full onslaught of summer and our one and only letter from Lena, written in the script of a five-year-old, her left hand not yet trained. She writes that rehabilitation is a silly word. She wants nothing of her former self. She says she will write again when she figures out what she wants to do. She never did, write that is. There are the reporters camped on our stairs, waiting for our daily journey to the courtroom. There is the courtroom where Heather sat, still beautiful, if not more so. Everyone says beauty comes from self-realisation. Piers and my father sit on opposite sides of the room and never speak a word to one another throughout the trial. Liv and my mother find each other in the Ladies room out of loyalty to their husbands, the last stall where they allow themselves to commiserate, to cry, to hold one another.

And then there is the last witness, Lena, wearing a turtleneck sweater. We all watch the video monitor as she gives her deposition. And, although the camera is trained on her face, I feel someone is holding her hand, which is making her uncomfortable. This will be the last time we will see her. We wait for another letter, but none comes. Eventually, my father will fly to New Orleans, but Lena has left the center weeks before. She had turned eighteen; there was nothing anyone could do to stop her. "Not that we would have. The girl knows her own mind," he is told. I've thought about this over the years. "Knows her own mind." And she never thought to tell us? The summer will end. And Heather will be sentenced to thirty years to life. She hasn't confessed. She hasn't given a reason. She hasn't finished high school.

I left as soon as I could and went to New York, where I met Marcelo. A year later, Mother followed with Frances. There was nothing left in Montreal for her. She meant her work had dried up. But she also claimed she never felt funny there, not funny enough. But the joke, in the end, was on her. Americans didn't get her British sense of humour. Editor after editor circled her copy and wrote in red pencil, "Is this supposed to be funny? I don't get it!!!"

My father would go to live in England for a time, but eventually went back to Canada, in large part because he hoped Lena might reappear. To mourn him is to know she was his last thought. She will be my last thought too.

You live in negative capability, C said to me when we were first falling in love. You live without knowing. Mother once confessed that she would often get the feeling that Lena was listening to her on the radio. I, too, each time I publish something, wonder if she's not tracking me. Google me. Here I am.

What time is it? Nearly six. The buses, even though it's not yet light, will be coming through soon. The man in the street knows it; he's picked himself up off the road where he went and sat when there was no threat of a passing car. I hope as he watches the buses rumble through that he feels by standing alone in the street he, for one night, escaped anonymity. It is Christmas morning.

I make my bed every morning, always shaking out the sheets, plumping the pillows, smoothing the bedspread, and wonder if I will live to unmake it. This day I have. But I hardly feel intact.

When C heard what had happened, he offered to fly home. But I told him, no. The panic is mostly gone, killed no doubt by this bottle of whiskey. It's more important that he finishes the rest of his research for his New York Times Magazine piece before returning here for the start of term. I hate my made bed. No, I hate that it is empty. Without C, what is a bed? I will have to call Frances. Not yet. I am afraid. Forgiveness looms, or at least, perhaps, an understanding, and I'm not ready for that.

None of this I could have suspected when C called me this morning, just like I could never have suspected that running into Beth at Yas Mall could so thoroughly alter the past and all my assumptions. Never assume. Isn't that what is said?

But it is what C said, what he told me this morning, that keeps banging around in my head. It was late in Brooklyn; he was jet-lagged, having flown in from South Africa the day before, me tracking his flight, all of them, in fact, AD to SA, SA to NY, my husband, a dot churning up and down the globe. All for his article on rogue elephants. In South Africa, the game warden drove him out to where the young elephant bulls, unmoored from any matriarchal guidance, did what many young men do when left to their own devices; go wilding. More than raping rhinos, they have been menacing those on safari, people who paid good money to see these wonders of nature—a world out of whack. The warden told him elephants are only hurting their cause. C saw the bulls, trumpeting, dashing headlong one way and then another. Those involved with the game reserve are of two minds. Some propose insinuating an elderly female elephant into their midst. Some want to break up the gang, dart them, drug them, and ship them off. All want something done before the next tourist season. But after this morning's visit with a neuroscientist at Rockefeller University, C thinks both schemes are probably next to useless.

"They don't understand."

"How could they?" I said, "You only started to understand today."

C nodded. I could see our Brooklyn apartment behind him. It looked so bare. I had given away all our plants and, in case any friends needed to use the place, put away in a drawer anything that might get broken, like the glass bowl C's mother left him and two Inuit statues, both at least a hundred years old, that had been given to my father after he delivered a 1930's Rolls Royce Phantom up to some mining magnate in James Bay. It is the only thing I have of his. Of course, as a kid, I dropped the male, and his leg broke off as did his harpoon. Both long lost now.

I noticed too that C had thrown his bag down on the floor, not bothering to unpack.

"How many brains did you see, anyway?"

"Lots. Big ones, little ones. They keep the brain of a whale in a garbage pail."

"That's too much gelatinous matter in a bucket for me."

"It was a bit...overwhelming. But think about it, Aug."

I have, I do.

C then picked up his laptop and went and sat by the

window so he could be more comfortable. My view now the distant lights of Manhattan.

"Spindle cells, they've been known about for a while. Though only recently, has it been proven that a baby, pretty much from birth, needs to have that constant connection, eye contact, the cooing sounds we make, and touch, touch is vital, basically a mother's love, or any love, for those cells to ignite."

"What do they look like?"

"Long, squiggly. Funny looking. We are born with them, but they need a lot of stimuli to get them going, to get them to the point that they start to migrate to the frontal lobe where they spark, well, all that's best about being mortal, empathy, the ability to love." C paused. I could hear an ambulance, it's siren wailing, pass on the street below, and only then did I realize that in all my time here, I have never heard a siren; police, fire, or ambulance. "Mortal, did you notice I said mortal, not human?"

I shook my head; I hadn't noticed.

"The hubris of humans yet again," C said, "In that cooler full of brains were the minds as magical, as feeling, as capable of empathy as ours. Whales have spindle cells, chimps, and elephants, Aug. Elephants! Those wilding bulls never had a chance. Their mothers were culled or murdered for their tusks when they were so young. I mean, it's just a theory, but what if all this aberrant behaviour, shit that's never been seen before is because they were denied the affection that ignites the spindle cells? What if that's the case?"

I saw C reach for his notebook. As I waited for him to jot down his note, I kept looking from the darkened

Brooklyn view to the blinding white Abu Dhabi one. The hotel under construction has a sign up written in Arabic but showing turtle hatchlings making the perilous journey from nest to sea. It's all a lie. The lights from the big hotels have disrupted millennia of mother turtles dragging themselves ashore and up the beach to lay and bury their eggs. Another thing dies out. When C looked up, I said, "Not snakes though, or turtles."

"Why do you say that?"

"They are hatched in the thousands. You said one needed a mother's love."

"Ok, maybe not reptiles. But who knows what they will find out. I would not be surprised if crows had them. Think about how smart they are?"

"And, they raise their chicks."

"Exactly!" C touched the screen. "You should be here," he said.

"I should."

"What will you do today?"

"I thought I'd go to the movies."

"Really?"

"I know it's a crazy thing to do on a Friday, but the walls are closing in."

"I'm think I should try and get some sleep."

"You should, night."

We both leaned into our computers at the same time and broke the connection. Did he stay like me, feeling almost silly that nine thousand miles could be gained and then severed so easily? Later, when I called again, I was close to hysterical, and he, still full of sleep, had trouble understanding what I was saying.

The drive out to Yas Mall is a small leap of faith, there are no exits once on the highway, and it's a good run caught between desert and Gulf. Yet you can see the workers camps, as well as hang gliders, or rather, water gliders, their arched sails zipping along just above sea and shore. In both cases, cars and buses must just turn off and bump over the sand, but I've never seen it. I no longer stay out of the fast lane. I've grown to like the thrill of looking through my rearview mirror at nothing one second and then the hawk lights of a Maserati or Ferrari crowding my view the next.

The mall on a Friday is filled with families, men having coffee, groups of teenagers, perfume hawkers, all making noise that should rise and dissipate but in the vast contained space becomes a numbing murmur which, in turn, flattens the scene around me. Lifeless. I walked through the crowds to the cinema. A bunch of teenage boys, rowdy even in their sparkling white dishdashas, were buying tickets to the same movie, so I left. Having abandoned more than a few movies because of the constant talking, texting, phoning, eating, C, and I have learned our lesson, see movies on a Tuesday or a Wednesday. What if I had gone in? I wanted to see the film, Brad Pitt's latest, a World War 11 spy drama. No. No more "what if's."

Her voice, calling to me, seemed impossible. I turned thinking, is it, Lena? I recognized Beth right away even though she was on the other side of the Mall's "Town Square." I stayed put as she threaded her way towards me. We hugged. I was surprisingly moved. And, was reluctant to let go.

When I did, Beth said right away that she was sorry she hadn't gotten in touch with me before. But her husband said he had upset me, so she didn't want to barge in.

Barge in?

She was still holding my hands though I was ready to let go.

"How are you? Really?" she asked.

"A little bummed." I said, "I wanted to see a movie, but..."

"Oh, never try to see movies Friday night."

"I know. I was foolish, but C is in New York, and I was..."

Beth squeezed my hands. "Bad time to be alone."

I felt my palms start to sweat. "Yes, well, it's a long time..."

"But coming on the heels of Liv's death."

I know all the expressions: the ground slipped away beneath her: the world began to spin; she couldn't catch her breath. They are all true. Ground slipped, world spun, breath left. Beth had to catch me.

There was only one question.

"Lena?"

"Let's get you..."

She led me to a Paul's. Got me to a table. Told the concerned waiter we needed tea and water.

"Lena?" I asked again.

Beth shook her head. "No."

I had an overwhelming urge to run away. But sat while the tea was brought. Beth took a sip and then leaned in, "Mary and I miss Leslie every day."

"Mary?"

"Mary, Leslie's best friend? You remember her, don't you?"

"Mary. Yes."

"We have a Leslie Memorial Club." Beth smiled. "It's really just the two of us. But once a year we get together and bake something in honour of Leslie. Last year it was cardamom cookies. It hasn't been easy for Mary. You remember the night Leslie was killed she was sent home because her mother wanted to tell Mary she had gotten engaged? Well, the guy turned out to be a real creep, if you know what I mean. Mary says she has scarring all along the inside of her cheek from the times he forced himself on her."

I tried to take a sip of my tea, but my hands were shaking too much.

"Isn't it strange that we both ended up here?" she said. "But how things end up is usually strange, isn't it?"

I nodded. Liv is dead. Does Lena know?

"Cassie was there, of course. But not Heather."

"Cassie?"

Beth clapped her hand over her mouth. "You don't know?"

"Know what?"

"Cassie is Heather's daughter."

"How?"

"Some guard, I think."

"She had a baby in prison?"

"No." Beth, aware now, and scared, knows she's holding a bomb. "She was released. Before."

"When?"

"Well, Cassie is in her thirties."

When I said nothing, what could I say? Beth went on.

"She was released. After five years. A model prisoner. And, you know how people reacted to her. She was pregnant. Like I said, a guard. Though she never said which one. That too swayed the parole board."

"How could I have not known?"

Beth looked at me. "I guess you had left. It was kept very quiet. I remember my mother talking to Liv in Wales during that period. She spent a fortune. Overseas calls in those days weren't cheap, but she had to be there for her friend. Liv was beside herself. She wasn't the one who was going to plead for them to keep her in prison. Piers wouldn't have allowed that, and it was her only surviving child."

"No, it wasn't. What the hell are you talking about!"

"Only child she knew her whereabouts. She didn't know where Lena was. Not after the letter..."

"What letter? Why didn't she write us?"

"I don't know. Please, Augati! You need to calm down. I only know what I know."

"What did she say to her mother?"

"I don't know exactly. My mother saw it, or Liv read it to her. I think she wrote the only way she was going to survive life, enough to have a life, was to be left alone. She would not be found."

"So, Liv never..."

"That was the last letter she ever got. She chose to respect Lena's wishes. Even if she knew others wouldn't."

"You mean me? My father? Her father? Maybe if we had had such a letter, we too could have been respectful! But we were left with nothing except confusion and the suspicion that any child gone wants to be found."

"Please, Augati, don't shout at me."

"Do you realize it consumed the last twenty years of my father's life?"

"I'm sorry to hear that," she said softly.

"Yeah, well."

Another round of tea arrived though I didn't see Beth order it. I dropped in two lumps of sugar, something I never do, but I didn't know what I was doing, and just stirred and stirred. It calmed me somewhat. There was a baby, a child, a woman now. I thought of the thrown down mattress', prison-like even back then. Did she invite the guard in? She must have.

"So Heather had a baby?" I said, not bothering to take a sip of my tea. It would cool untouched.

"Yes, and right after she abandoned her."

"Abandoned her?"

"She had no interest in raising her. Liv and Piers took her."

"Liv raised her?"

"I think it helped with the healing process."

"What?"

"It wasn't easy. My mother told me that Liv, especially when Cassie hit adolescence, lived in terror that she would exhibit some of the same characteristics as Heather."

"You mean she was scared that Cassie might be a psychopathic murdering bitch?"

Beth looked down at her tea. "I think she meant subtler problems. Hoarding, detachment."

"Cassie? Short for Cassandra?"

"I guess."

"I wouldn't have thought Heather would have so ironic a sense of humour."

"I don't think she named her. It was Liv."

Heather had killed beauty for me. I see only the fear of being so coveted or the madness brought on by the power of it.

"Is she weirdly beautiful like Heather?"

"No. Not that she isn't lovely. Or at least she is in the pictures I've seen of her. But not otherworldly. My mother went to Wales a couple of times over the years to see Liv, to offer support. Liv grappled with a lot of guilt. Cassie knew nothing of her mother's past. Still doesn't as far as I know."

"How is that even possible?"

"She lives in Wales, and it was a long time ago. I mean, one could ask how come no-one ever found Lena?"

I didn't point out that Liv chose not to look for her and, I knew if I mentioned again my father, broken each time the search came up empty, I might start crying.

"And Heather?"

"This makes me so angry." Beth pursed her lips. "Heather, Heather, if you can believe this has lived all these years, well, mostly in Florida, the mistress to a succession of rich yacht owners..."

My laughter caught me unawares, and I couldn't stop. I saw it all: the rich fucks, the sultry Miami heat, the mysterious woman who might take that ship's tackle and drive it through your skull. You don't have yachts and wealth unless you are willing to gamble. She must seem to them the ultimate roulette game. It is all too sordid. Her beauty was such that's she's probably still at it, a little leathery around the edges, but the age of the suiters probably has edged up too. And she would be cruel enough to demand the extra doses of viagra and not mind a little droop as long as he held up his end of the bargain. I bet she feels that she put one over all of us. I got up then.

Beth walked me to my car and made me promise to wait while she got hers so she could follow me home. I watched her in my rear view, close behind, but not in the fast lane. At my exit, I put on my signal and raised my hand. She flashed her lights.

Now, this bourbon, the tea taste long gone, keeps bringing me back to what C said earlier today about the brain. About empathy and contact. It keeps bringing me to Heather.

Much was made at the trial about her origins, which created a storm of protest and forced both the Crown prosecution and the defence to tread carefully. The whole nature/nurture argument was coming to the fore. How then to present the luckless start of being abandoned by what was assumed to be a strung-out teenager in Channel-Port aux Basques. She was found in the bathroom of a bar. (God help me, but I remember during the trial thinking if she weren't a psycho killer, she would have had the most romantic beginnings) When no one came forward to claim her, she was shipped off to an orphanage run by nuns, I forget which order, where she languished until Liv and Piers showed up in St John's. She was nearly three. Leslie was a newborn.

At the trial, the prosecution roared that Heather Driscoll had been given every opportunity despite her beginnings and that there was no way to look at what she had done in any other light then cold, calculated murder!"

The defence, on the other hand, posited that there

was no manifest destiny; we are slaves to our biological impulses. And that scared the hell out of people. We were not so far north of the sixties and the belief of taking control, giving free love, taking free love, fighting the man. And, no one yet was steeped in terms like Detachment disorder, and PTSD. Now I imagine there isn't a killer out there who doesn't have a defence team rocking the juries' initial prejudices with all that the brain can suffer before we've even found language and had our first thought.

And, now, C has given me spindle cells. I can't help but think of all those Romanian orphans that were snapped up after Ceausescu, and his wife Elena were put up against a wall and riddled with bullets. Babies who couldn't make eye contact, couldn't bond, couldn't understand affection, or baby talk all because they had rarely been touched, or sang too. No one had looked them in the eye with enough maternal love that their dormant spindle cells could do what they were supposed to do, migrate and create the desire for concourse with other humans and foster the natural urge to be empathetic.

Add Heather to that list.

Fuck.

So, an answer, a possible explanation for that day. I hate it. I don't want it. I don't want to see a pretty little baby lying in a cot, her tiny hands reaching to find only air, her curious eye seeking and finding no stimuli other than some shitty donated mobile spinning ceaselessly above her head. Her days marked by a wimple (if that's what those nuns wore) and a dour face, changing and feeding her quickly as they were rushed. There were lots of other babies.

Eventually, though, came new faces. I see Piers, not lifting her with love but assessment, wanting to make sure she was a perfectly healthy baby. It was Liv who spotted Leslie two cots over and had to have her too, a weak, sick child, who hadn't yet opened her eyes. So even that moment was robbed from Heather. In the long trip home, where Liv worried because Leslie didn't cry, didn't fuss while Heather (their names chosen at the Orphanage) was held awkwardly by Piers. What would it have taken to make Heather's spindle cells spring into action? (This I have no doubt is too reductive, being a murderer can't just be based on a few cells, but nothing else makes sense) Something more, I imagine, than a cold man staring out a train window wondering how he had been roped into taking two babies. Something more than a suddenly harried mother. (One to three children overnight) Something more than a new sister like Lena, who I, myself, spent my youth trying to get her to turn her attention to me. What must she have been like with Heather? There was a photo shown at the trial of the day they met. Liv is leading Heather and Lena into their new bedroom with matching twin beds (one red, one blue) and a shelf with one of each sort of toy, a teddy bear, a doll, a book, leading her little girls into a world of rigid sharing, canned love, a mock-up of a family. Lena never complained about having to share a bedroom but always kept her love neatly packed away. Self-preservation.

Heather never had a chance. None of us did. Her beauty didn't save her, probably the opposite, the attraction it created: invasive, even nonsensical to a mind that couldn't read the clues of love, compassion. A mind built

175

only to deliver shocks: a raised skirt, a violated textbook, a smashed picture, an ax to the head.

I am sick with sadness. Understanding the biological routes to who we are leaves us all prisoners. I want to crawl now into my made bed, but the dogs are staring at me. It's dawn, and they have waited through this night, never quite sleeping. I have to take them out.

It is a silent morning in this marooned city. The dogs' noses are twitching. A cat must have just passed. There are no clouds in the sky. I look to my windsock. But it's not there. Another thing taken. The prevailing winds are lost to me now, and I have no twitchy receptors with which to pick up the subtle signals from this blanched landscape.

I feel different. Heavier somehow. Have since I spoke to C and bumped into Beth. I think I know what it is, this new weight. The weight of knowledge. And it is one I will carry for you, Lena, because I can, and, with that, I'll let you go. The search is over.

ACKNOWLEDGEMENTS

First, I'd like to thank, with every fibre of my being, technology. For most of my writing career, I was hamstrung by learning disabilities, and I required an enormous amount of help from my husband, Charles. He had to proofread everything I wrote and make sense of the tangled madness that my dyslexic brain came up with. Now with tools like Grammarly, talk/text, and Ghostreader, he is finally a free man.

I would also like to thank my cousin Imogen, an ace copy editor, who combed through the book and found all the small inconsistencies that no technology would ever have picked up on.

It's been a while since I've published a book, and god knows when the next one will come out, so I want to thank everyone. Literally. Frank, who has been my best friend for more than 40 years. His lovely wife, Jovi. And, of course, Azalea. John, Mary, Ray, and Sophia, my second family. My pals Rebecca and Andrew. The inimitable Jane. Chris, who took me on fantastic world travels. Judy, my one-time editor and dear friend. Neil, who tried for many years. All the Siebert's and their spouses. The far-flung, Jon Lee and Erica. Manny, who, by asking me to write "anything I want" for Salon, allowed me to pin down the tone I needed. Aimee Lee Ball, who allowed me to circle around my relationship with my mother. To Scott and Nanette. Michelle, an early reader of one of the many iterations of the book. Jeff, who was always weirdly optimistic about my career. To the French gang, Mary, Gretchen, and Susan. Deborah, my Abu Dhabi compatriot. My other cousins, Helen, Connie, Jess, Danielle and Anne. To my stepmother Carol. Santiago and Frankie and, of course, David. My sisters Tina, Mercy, and Sophie, obviously, this book would not have any spine at all them without them. Tod and Spuyten Duyvil Press. And lastly, my aforementioned husband, Charles. We always joked about acknowledgments and swore we'd never say, "Without you, this book wouldn't have been written." So I won't, but it wouldn't have.

BEX BRIAN lives mostly in Brooklyn with her husband, the writer Charles Siebert and their dog, Olive. She's been scribbling around on various projects for the better part of thirty years. *Radius* is her second novel.

CPSIA information can be obtained
at www.ICGtesting.com
Printed in the USA
LVHW041557161220
674342LV00014B/2881